LUNCHMEAT LENNY

6th Grade Crime Boss

Story One—The Extraordinary Crew

By

DANIEL KENNEY

This book is dedicated to my boys

CHAPTER ONE

My name is Lenny Parker and I already know what you're thinking. I don't look anything like that tough kid on the cover, do I? Well, there's an explanation for that. In fact, there's an explanation for practically everything. You see, I never meant to be a crime boss. I just wanted my peanut butter back.

My dad, the Colonel, had moved Mom and me to Wedge City, California, and I was starting my sixth school in six years. The Colonel promised this move would be different, that we might actually stay a few years. And, the Colonel pointed out two more advantages to our new hometown.

First, we'd be only three hours north of San Francisco and the Colonel promised he'd take me to see my beloved San Francisco Giants for the very first time. Second, a brand new amusement park called Danger Mountain was being built just outside of town. Inside of this man-made mountain was going to be a full amusement park complete with a first of its kind mining tunnel rollercoaster. In other words, about the most awesome thing I could imagine.

And so, during the first week of August, the Colonel, my mom, and I moved from Nevada to Northern California. Correction, my mom and I did most of the moving while the Colonel drove ahead so he could take over his new command at Gardner Army Base. And within a few short days, I'd already attended my first day of school.

My new school was McMillan, a huge rectangular red brick building in the center of town with a tall flagpole out front. I suppose it was like the other six schools I'd attended in my life with the exception that it was bigger. And meaner. I was in sixth grade now. I had a locker, walked to all my classes, and saw things I'd never seen before in my life.

On the first day, I walked into the stairwell to see three eighth grade girls giving each other homemade tattoos. One of them growled and told me to move before she kicked me where "the sun don't shine." I didn't want to find out where exactly the "sun don't shine," so I scurried away fast. Another day, I saw a boy with a Mohawk start a trash can on fire in the library, then drop it out of the second-story window where it fell onto the principal's car. And on yet another day, I saw that same boy skateboard down the middle of a cafeteria table filled with girls. By the time he reached the other side of the cafeteria, the school's Head of Discipline, Helmet Kruger, had his hands around the boy, dragging him off to detention.

The boy's name was Eddie, but people called him Spaghetti Eddie. In addition to his weird nickname and strange hairdo, he always wore a long black trench coat, skateboarded to every class, and had what the Colonel would call a bad attitude. I knew because he smarted off in our math class all the time and got detentions on an almost daily basis. In fact, Spaghetti Eddie was everything the Colonel despised and maybe for that reason, I was strangely curious about him.

But I stayed my distance. I always stayed my distance. In the past, I'd made the mistake of making friends only to find out that the Colonel was moving me to yet another town and another school.

I stopped making that mistake three schools ago. Now, I did my time. I stayed out of trouble, tried to get B's, and followed my number one rule.

Never make friends.

I know what you're thinking, how's a kid get along without friends? Not as hard as you think. My mom's nice and she pretty much lets me do what I want. And for a couple of moves I had a pet bullfrog named Cinnamon. That was fun until one night Cinnamon got away from his aquarium, and decided to sleep in the blender. And the next morning when mom went to make her smoothie? Let's just say it was Cinnamon flavored. Not pretty. I've been somewhat traumatized ever since, mom even made me go see a therapist because of the whole thing. I think he diagnosed me with post-traumatic frog disorder.

But thankfully, through it all; through the constant moves, the different schools, the dad who's never there and the exploding bullfrog; there's always been one constant. The one thing I could always count on: beautiful brown color, smooth creamy texture, and deep rich taste.

Peanut butter.

You see, I'm a picky eater. There's not much I eat. But I've always loved peanut butter. Some kids get handed a football or a baseball when they're babies. I think I must have had a spoonful of extra creamy in my crib.

Peanut Butter is the perfect food really. It's a nut and an oil. There's sugar in it, and tons of protein and fat. I do eat other foods. Bread, crackers, basically anything that can act as a peanut butter delivery mechanism. I learned delivery mechanism in some ballistic missile documentary the Colonel made me watch.

One time, we were out of bread at the house, so I cut up pieces of a Nike shoe box and had myself a cardboard peanut butter sandwich. Not as bad as you think. Mom thought I was crazy, but then I showed her the box and the secret message the box had given me. "Mom," I whispered. "The box told me to just do it. So *I did.*"

It didn't take me long to fall into a familiar pattern in my unfamiliar town. Every day, I would ride my bike home from school. It gave me a chance to see a little bit of the new town I was in. When I got home every day, I'd fix myself a couple peanut butter sandwiches, do my homework, then watch baseball on the television. And then I would wait. Mom and I would both wait for the Colonel to get home and if he did, he would tell us about how important his job was, and how he knew we understood, and about how hopefully I would grow into the type of man who one day makes him proud.

And sometimes he would look at me and sort of shake his head.

And when I was certain my parents were in bed for the night, I usually would slip down to the kitchen, eat peanut butter straight out of the jar, stare out the window, and wonder whether next year, the next town, and the next school would finally be different.

CHAPTER TWO

On the Monday of my second week at McMillan, I walked from Algebra to Social Studies while focused on a pair of green tennis shoes six feet in front of me. Somebody bumped me from the left. "It's Lenny right?"

I looked over. A girl. She had ridiculous long brown hair that she kept in pig tails, she wore bright blue overalls, had strange looking glasses, and exceptionally big teeth. And she was talking. To me.

"Yes," I said, then put my head back down.

"I'm Megan. But most people call me Mega Bits."

I kept following the green shoes.

"Aren't you going to ask me why?" she asked.

"Not really," I said, keeping my eyes focused on the floor in front of me.

"I'm good with computers." She shrugged. "I guess you could call me a computer genius."

I looked over again and she smiled, her teeth somehow even bigger than I observed the first time. Her upper lip was thin and her lower lip was big. Like they were mismatched.

"Computers have bytes and bits and all that jazz, so that's where it comes from."

"Oh," I managed to finally say.

"So, you're new and I noticed you eating alone during lunch. You should come sit with me and my friends."

I stood in front of Mrs. Hardy's science class and Megan, or whatever she called herself, was bouncing up and down on her tiptoes apparently waiting for me to talk.

"Yeah, well I've got to go," I said, then slipped into class before she could even respond.

I sat alone at lunch and avoided Mega Bits every time she tried to catch my eye. Instead, I focused on my double peanut butter sandwich and the Reese's

Peanut Butter Cup I snuck out of my mom's purse. After school, I rode my bike home like usual, but took a detour down Main Street when I noticed a kid with a Mohawk screaming down the middle of the street on his skateboard. Spaghetti Eddie. I followed him down Main Street, and watched as he weaved in and out of cars, hopped onto the curb, jumped his board up onto a planter box, flipped the red and black skateboard into the air, and landed squarely back down on it.

Then Spaghetti Eddie sailed down the sidewalk, his long black trench coat flowing behind him so that you couldn't even see the board and it looked like he was floating sideways down the sidewalk. He was heading for Maple's News Stand and crouched low to the ground as he approached. And as he passed by the front of the newsstand, he reached his hand up, and grabbed a candy bar. Then he kept riding down the street. Mr. Maple never even saw him.

No doubt about it, the Colonel would *definitely* not like Spaghetti Eddie. But me? Had to admit. Still curious.

I kept following him and watched him turn down an alley. I waited a bit, then turned down the alley myself. As soon as I did, something hit me hard and I flew off my bike. I scrambled to get up, but Eddie stepped over me and set his boot onto my chest. He reached in his trench coat, pulled out an enormous alarm clock, wound it up, and set it next to me on the ground.

"You've got thirty seconds to explain."

"Explain what?" I said.

"Why you're following me."

The clock ticked loudly. I squirmed, but Eddie pressed his boot down harder.

"I was curious," I gurgled out.

"About?" he said.

"Who you are and what you do."

"So you're not with the Irish gang?"

"The what?" I said.

"You're not with the Irish?"

"I don't know what you're talking about. My name is Lenny, I'm new in school, and my dad's a Colonel in the army."

Eddie loosened the pressure on my chest. He shook his head.

"I see you follow me again, and I'll hurt you. Got it?"

He grabbed his skateboard, jumped on board, and took off, his trench coat flowing behind him, his dark Mohawk fading in the distance.

I stumbled to my feet, found my bike, and peddled like crazy for home.

 # CHAPTER THREE

"So, I invite you to my table and you decide to eat by yourself instead?" I looked up. It was Mega Bits. Big teeth.

I shrugged.

"Don't worry, I've decided that since you won't eat with us, I will eat with you today." She sat.

"I'm fine by myself, okay?"

Mega Bits paused, folded her hands and leaned forward.

"Are you? Are you fine by yourself? We get kids like you every year. Your dad's in the military isn't he?"

I paused. "How did you know that?"

"Listen, Lenny, you dress like one of the Hardy boys. You're the only kid in school who has a crease in his khakis and wears short sleeve button-down shirts. I'm guessing your dad is a Colonel, right?"

"You're a good guesser."

"Ha, I didn't guess. I looked you up. You've been to a different school for the last six years. That's a drag."

"You looked me up?" I said, more than a little annoyed.

"So let me ask you—the whole walk around with your head down all the time, is that a defense mechanism or just a sign of low self-esteem?"

"You looked me up?" I said again.

She made a face and pushed against her glasses with her finger. "And I've been watching you. Every day, a peanut butter sandwich and a plastic baggie full of peanut butter that you eat with your finger. A little disgusting and, more to the point, just plain weird."

"Why are you watching me?"

"Lenny, you're not helping yourself out here. You may have been able to get away with this act before, but you're in Junior High now. Junior High is the show. I hear there are bets being placed right now on which guy's going to stuff you into a locker first."

I'd never been stuffed into a locker before. Maybe she was kidding. "Just leave me alone. I'll be fine."

She leaned back in her chair, folded her arms, and got a curious look on her face. "So that's it, isn't it? You try to act invisible. You figure if you don't look at anybody or offend anybody and just keep to yourself—that you'll be fine until the next time your daddy moves."

I stiffened. My face grew warm and my hand clenched around my sandwich. "And *you* can somehow help me?"

She scrunched up her chin. "I can. I'll lead you around, introduce you to people, help you make friends." She jabbed a thumb at her chest. "You stick with me, sixth grade will be a lot more enjoyable."

I looked over at her normal table. Two nerdy girls sat there, giggling over a math book. I shook my head at Mega Bits.

"Not so sure taking advice from you is such a good idea."

Her face fell, her mouth hanging half open. Then she glared at me and sprung up.

"I thought you might be different, but Lenny, you're no better than the rest of them."

 # CHAPTER FOUR

I avoided Mega Bits the rest of the week, and on Friday raced home after school to get ready. It was the last Giant's game that might work with the Colonel's busy schedule, and he promised to get home early so we could make it to San Francisco on time.

Did I mention the Colonel's not very good at keeping promises? I and my glove waited for him on the front porch and, of course, he never came. Mom eventually came outside to break the news that the Colonel had to work late that night doing maneuvers, whatever those were.

"Sorry bout last night, Lenny," the Colonel said the next morning when I came down to the kitchen. He was polishing his boots. I'm not sure he even looked up when he said it.

I shrugged and walked away. "It's just disappointing," I muttered.

I probably shouldn't have used that word.

"Excuse me," he said in the voice that meant I better stop and look at him immediately. "Disappointing?" he said. He shook his head, snorted, then went back to spit polishing his boots. "Well that's just rich. Lenny, you don't know the meaning of disappointment. Have you ever spent a whole summer in the filthy hot jungle? Ninety-eight days in a row I ate canned tuna on saltine crackers. On day ninety-nine, I ran out of tuna so I spent the day gnawing on my finger. You know what disappointment is? Day one hundred. I was still hungry but in addition to not having food, now I didn't have my finger." He held up his ring finger, the one that was half as long as the others. "You ever experience disappointment like that?"

I was only twelve years old, had never been in the jungle, and had all ten of my fingers. So I guess the Colonel had a point. He also had on his army face. My dad wasn't a yeller. He had perfected this "I'm disappointed in you" face that I called his Army face. What it meant was somebody, usually me, was not up to army standards. His standards.

In fact, I so consistently failed to measure up to Army standards, that I wasn't entirely sure why the Colonel kept me around. He should have adopted a first lieutenant or a shiny green jeep instead. I remember one day in particular, Dad was trying to help me think of things I was good at for a school project. Noticeably stumped, he whacked me on the shoulder. "Well, at least you're the son of a Colonel, so you've got that going for you."

He actually said that to me.

Maybe that's why I started to love peanut butter so much.

And that's also why the Colonel doesn't really need to know about this crime boss thing. Not yet. Maybe when he's real old, and he's using a cane, and wearing an eye patch, and he no longer carries a gun on his waist, and he's hooked up to an oxygen tank, maybe then I'll tell him all about how his son became Lunchmeat Lenny and how I found my extraordinary crew.

The day after the Colonel forgot to take me to the Giants game, he broke more bad news. He had to make an emergency trip overseas. Didn't know for sure when he'd be back, but it would probably be a month at least.

And just like that, Mom and I were alone once more. That night, I snuck down to the kitchen, ate peanut butter from the jar and looked outside. And in the morning, I woke up early, and made my famous peanut butter pancakes. Then before I left for school, I reminded Mom that I just finished up the last of the peanut butter, and handed her a double coupon I'd found in the newspaper.

She smiled and assured me that the pantry would be well stocked by the time I returned from school.

# CHAPTER FIVE

School was mostly normal that day, except for the commotion in the cafeteria. Some emergency that I didn't know anything about, nor did I care. Normally by the end of a school day, I have serious peanut butter on the brain, I can't think or concentrate on anything else, and I ride my bike home as fast as possible.

That's what I did on this day, but while I weaved in and out of cars, jumped curbs and avoided women with strollers, I noticed something strange. Big green cargo vans were everywhere. And coming out of houses carrying cardboard boxes were guys wearing blue suits and wearing silver sunglasses. It was weird and any other time, I might have cared. But like I said, when PB is on the brain, I'm all in. And I needed to get home.

I noticed a couple more of those green vans on my street, but blew past them, rode into my driveway, and dropped my bike against our front steps. I rushed into the house and ran for the kitchen. Mom was sitting alone at the kitchen table. She looked up and in an instant, I knew. Something was wrong.

She was holding the afternoon paper and had an empty look in her eye. Her lower lip trembled. There was a single tear on her cheek.

Something terrible had happened.

"Lenny?"

"Mom, whatever it is can't be too bad, just let me fix myself a sandwich and then we can talk about it."

All of a sudden, my mom jumped up like a jack-in-the-box and stood in front of me and the pantry. This was weird behavior, especially for my mom.

"Err, Mom, would you mind moving?"

Droplets of sweat collected on her forehead.

"Lenny, you know what I was thinking, why eat peanut butter today? Why not change things up? How about today I take you out for a big hot fudge sundae?"

But Mom wasn't smiling when she said it. She was chewing on the corner of her lip so hard it was starting to bleed. Something was not right.

"You're freaking me out, Mom. After my sandwich we can talk, but I'm starting to get a little dizzy, I need to eat." I reached my hand over her shoulder and grabbed hold of the cabinet door knob.

That's when Mom turned into a crazy person. She grabbed me around the waist in a bear hug and started to lift me away from the pantry. Luckily, I had a good grip and I wasn't about to let go of that door.

She yelled at me to let go, then when that wouldn't work—"don't do it Lenny! Let's go out for ice cream, ice cream is so much better than peanut butter. Or chocolate, how about you just start eating chocolate instead?!"

I kept pulling.

"Or, I could just dump sugar right down your throat, please, Lenny?!"

It's like aliens had abducted my mother, and this lady who was holding onto me was some freakishly strong impostor. At least that's the rationale I used when I did something that I'm not terribly proud of.

I kicked my mom. Hard. Right in the shin. She let go of me immediately, squealed like a stuck pig, and then started hopping around on one foot. Like I said, not proud of it. But at the moment, she was the psycho alien creature keeping a hungry boy away from his peanut butter and I didn't know what else to do.

I opened up the pantry, looked inside, and I felt like I got punched in the gut.

On the left were the boxes of cereal. On the right were the cans of vegetables. But in the middle, the grand middle where the peanut butter was always featured?

Nothing.

No peanut butter. Not one jar. Just a bunch of empty shelf space, mocking me.

Mom had never, and I mean never, forgotten to buy peanut butter before, and that meant something terrible really had occurred. I spun around and mom was just shaking her head, holding onto the newspaper.

"Mom," I said, my voice a little shaky. "Why is there no peanut butter in the pantry?"

She shook her head back and forth, then looked at me with her big brown eyes. "Lenny, I'm just so sorry, I don't know what to say. I went to the grocery store today, and when I did, there were vans outside, a bunch of men in blue suits carrying out boxes and boxes of...." She swallowed hard and started to let out a full-throated sob.

"Peanut butter, Lenny. They were taking it all. I asked the store manager what was going on. He looked at me like I was crazy. 'Haven't you heard what happened?' he said. Then he handed me a newspaper and when I read the headline, I thought I might get sick."

My head was spinning at the possibilities.

"Lenny, I'm sorry. I feel so bad for you."

"What mom, what exactly happened?"

She handed me the newspaper. On the front page in huge block letters was the headline.

I stumbled back in horror, then gathered myself, and read the headline again:

NATIONAL FOOD EMERGENCY
PEANUT BUTTER NO LONGER SAFE

CHAPTER SIX

I screamed for a few minutes, then fell to the floor where I sat crisscross, and made pretend peanut butter sandwiches for the next hour. At least that's what Mom tells me. I can't remember anything. The base doctor eventually came over and utilized what he explained to my mom was the latest medical therapy for dealing with shock. Mom said it looked like he dropped a couple ice cubes down my shorts. Regardless, it was effective and I and my wet butt were alert for the next hour as Mom told the doctor about every runny nose and headache I'd ever had in my life. She even told him about the frog in the blender incident. The doctor explained that a combination post traumatic frog *and* peanut butter disorder was highly unusual; it was more likely that I was just plain weird.

Mom kept me home from school the next day; tried feeding me cereal, toast, and Jell-O. I licked a bowl of corn flakes for a while, threw the toast around my room like a Frisbee and soaked my foot in Cherry Jell-O (which if you've never done it, feels surprisingly good). But I wasn't about to eat any of it. My heart was broken.

All I could think about was peanut butter, and why anyone would make the most brilliant food in the world illegal. You might as well tell people to stop gazing upon Michelangelo's Sistine Chapel, to stop walking to the foot of the Great Pyramids of Giza, or to stop reading The Beef Jerky Gang. I mean, who denies people an encounter with perfection?

Guys wearing blue suits and silver sunglasses, that's who. And the whole *national food emergency* made no sense. I knew peanut butter better than anybody alive and didn't believe for a second it was unsafe. Something weird was going on.

If I was more like my dad, I'd track down those blue suit guys, find out what was going on, and get my peanut butter back. But I wasn't like my dad. My dad was a Colonel, a leader of men. I was a weird kid with an unhealthy food obsession and no friends. The only thing I truly excelled at was disappointing my dad.

I stared through the mini-blinds that covered my windows and caught the half-moon that hung over the night sky. The Colonel didn't like half-moons. Said the only acceptable moons were full. Those half-moons lacked commitment and lack of commitment was the sign of a weak mind. Certainly not fit for the Army way. I had the distinct feeling the Colonel wasn't talking about moons.

The next day, I convinced Mom that my body needed to stay immobile in order to adjust to living in a reality that included the absence of a certain delectable food spread. She said I could stay in bed, but only if I promised to eat toast and jam. I agreed, then dutifully tore the toast apart from its crusts, hid it in an old pair of shoes, and gave the crusts back to mom. She was proud that I was developing an appetite for new food.

By day three, it was getting harder to convince mom to let me stay home from school. She said that I needed to get out of the house, or she would be forced to call the Colonel and get him involved. I countered by saying that I would get out of bed and even out of the house but needed one more day of acclimating my new body chemistry to the world before heading back to school. She agreed and by late morning, I had pretended to eat my morning toast and was ready to leave.

CHAPTER SEVEN

I rode my bike down to Main Street and cruised past the shops. On the right was a comic book store, a few clothing stores, a collectible shop, and a bar. On the left was a dry cleaners, a jewelry store, and an Italian restaurant named Pellano's. Two large men stood outside the restaurant, their hands folded in front of them. They wore dark suits, even darker sunglasses and looked more like small mountains than men. I kept moving.

I kept rolling down Main Street when I saw movement to my right. A man in a blue suit and silver sunglasses carrying a cardboard box into the back of a green van. I stopped. The door to the back of the van was open, and inside were stacks and stacks of something brown and beautiful.

Peanut butter.

My hand started to shake and my mouth began to water. The man stepped back out of the van, and walked back to a storefront. The van remained there, alone. The back doors were open and all of that peanut butter just sat there.

I hadn't had any peanut butter in days. Days. And at this rate, I might never have peanut butter again until ... well, I didn't know when. A noise off to my right caught my attention and I turned. A skateboard rolled past ridden by a tall skinny kid with long blonde hair.

I thought of Spaghetti Eddie, and remembered seeing him steal that candy bar from Maple's newsstand.

He had made it look so easy.

I had an idea. A crazy idea. And I didn't have time to debate my crazy idea. I had a chance, and no matter how wrong it might be, I'd rather be wrong than hungry. I slammed my foot down on the pedal, and started riding like mad for the back of that van. If I could only reach it before that blue-suit guy got back. I was getting closer, getting closer, closer. I skidded to a stop, jumped off and found myself at the back of the van. I'd never been that close to so much peanut butter that in all my life. I took a deep breath, reached out my hand, and my neck jerked back hard.

Something large and strong, like an earth mover, grabbed the back of my collar and lifted me straight into the air. "Got the little waste-oid, Vince." A voice behind me crackled into a radio while a gigantic fist held me. He had turned me around and was walking me away from the van. He grabbed my bike with his other hand and walked both of us toward a large black SUV. He opened the back trunk with his teeth, then tossed both me and my bike into the trunk and slammed the door shut. The driver spun the wheels of the truck, pulled a U-turn and raced a couple blocks down the street until he stopped. Right in front of that Italian Restaurant. Pellano's.

The door swung open and my new personal guard yanked me out. He dragged me to the front door of the restaurant and sat me down in front of another enormous dude, who immediately put both hands on my shoulders and frisked me.

He opened his mouth, as if to show off the sparkly gold tooth in the middle of his smile. "If you've got a weapon, better to tell me now. I find it on my own, and I'll have to break both your kneecaps. Company policy."

"And if you find out from me?" my voice cracked.

"I only break one kneecap." He smiled again, sunlight dancing off that gold tooth. Had to admire a guy who enjoyed his job so much.

"I've got no weapon," I said.

He reached down the front pocket of my khaki pants.

"Well, what do we have here?" he said, while unfolding a piece of paper.

The guard behind me tugged on my collar, the shirt wrenching against my throat and cutting off my oxygen.

"That's a double coupon for peanut butter," I squeaked. "It's good until the end of the month."

He squinted his eyes at me.

"Right," he said sarcastically. "What's it really? Some secret spy stuff from Ears Malone?"

"Ears Malone?" I said.

"You look like the kind of little kid he might use for his dirty work. Those Irish got no principles 'bout using kids."

The guy behind me pulled harder on my collar. I had to squeeze out the words.

"I'm part Dutch, part German, with a tiny bit of French mixed in."

The guy with the gold tooth laughed. "That's funny kid, but let's be clear, don't try to be funny in there." He nodded towards the restaurant. "And kid, you're already in enough trouble, so whatever you do, don't ever stare Scar's goldfish in the eye."

"Scar? A goldfish? Are you joking with me?"

The man scowled. "Scar never jokes about his goldfish."

CHAPTER EIGHT

My personal guard pushed me through the door and I was assaulted with an explosion of Italian scents. Like spaghetti sauce and Parmesan cheese were conspiring to overthrow my digestive system. Four days with barely any food was starting to seriously mess with me.

A heavy Italian woman was on the phone behind a counter, yelling at someone named Niko. She rolled her eyes when she saw me then made a little sign of the cross on her forehead. Not comforting.

I was marched up a large staircase to the second floor, where another mountain of a man waited by a door. My personal guard leaned in and whispered something. Mr. Mountain gave me the kind of look they give you in movies when you're about to walk into a room with a very large monster. Then he pushed up his lips and nose and stepped aside.

I entered a private dining room occupied by large, dark-suited men eating, laughing, and slapping each other on the backs. Near the rear of the room was a long rectangular table. The scariest man I'd ever seen stood in the middle. A pink scar zig-zagged down his right cheek. Behind him stood an enormous aquarium with a goldfish the size of a soccer ball. To my greater surprise, this goldfish had only one eye. For a moment I was mesmerized. But only for a moment. I remembered what those goons told me about staring.

Scar Pellano was busy lecturing another man about responsibilities, debts, and loyalty. The man wore a dirty white apron and stood in the center of the room. His legs were shaking and he was having a difficult time focusing on Mr. Pellano. His attention was being drawn away from Scar by that giant one-eyed goldfish.

Finally, Scar pounded his fist on the table.

"Am I boring you, Mr. Matthews?"

The man shook even more. "Err, no sir."

"Because it seems like you'd rather look at my goldfish than listen to me."

"No, Scar, honest—"

Scar pounded his fist on the table again.

"Nobody, and I mean nobody, looks my goldfish in the eye."

The man started sobbing into his hands.

"I'm sorry, Scar, I meant nothing by it. Just that eye is so big, I couldn't help it...."

I saw Scar's hand move under the table.

"Do you know what happens to people who fall through my trap door?"

The man looked down at his feet and that's when I saw it. He was standing on a red 'x' and around him was a black circle. He held up his hands and waved them.

"No, Scar, don't. Don't! I'll do anything, anything." He crumpled to the ground and began sobbing."

Scar's hand slid further under the table. He opened his mouth and showed his teeth. "Goodbye, Mr. Matthews."

Mr. Matthews threw his hands up again and screamed.

Scar stopped and shrugged.

"Or, maybe not. Maybe, just maybe you learned your lesson this time, what do ya think?"

Mr. Matthews was trembling as his eyes darted around the room. He wiped his mouth and stood up, body shaking hard.

"Oh yes, yes sir, Mr. Scar. I most definitely learned my lesson. It will never, and I mean never, happen again."

Scar leaned over the table, and gripped the edges hard. "It better not." He nodded to one of his men who grabbed Mr. Matthews by the arm and dragged him past me. My personal guard pushed me from behind and positioned me on the 'x', where just seconds before poor Mr. Matthews had stood. Then he moved over to Scar and whispered something to his boss. Scar listened with one ear, and nodded his head, then he took a big drink of wine. Without even looking at me, Scar extended a big stubby finger my direction, and started jabbing at the air.

He rose from the table.

"You sure you're not one of Malone's kids? Those Irish punks like to send kids to do their dirty work."

"I'm Dutch and German, not an ounce of Irish in me."

Scar slapped the table and snorted.

"And does '*Mr. Not an ounce of Irish in me*' have a name."

"My name's Lenny."

"Lenny?" Scar scratched his chin, and he looked to his left and to his right. "I don't think that's possible."

"No, really my name is Lenny," I said.

"I don't think that's possible because I don't remember ever giving any Lenny permission to pull jobs in my city."

I didn't really understand what Scar just said.

"And yet here you are, a kid named Lenny, and my boys catch you on Main Street, trying to steal Peanut Butter out of the back of a van, am I right?"

"No, sir, it's not that simple—"

He cut me off with a wave of his hand. "Not that simple," he growled. He pointed at me. "You, a kid I never met before, lecturing me on what is and isn't simple?" Scar flared his nose and reached his hand underneath the table like he had with Mr. Matthews.

I jumped up.

"You heard about what happened with peanut butter right?" I said.

"Kid, I run this town. Course I heard about it."

"I want to get some."

"Some what?" Scar said.

"Peanut butter. I want to get some peanut butter."

"So you're looking to score more than one jar?"

"Score?" I asked.

"And is there a reason you didn't get my permission first?" Scar said.

"I don't know what you're talking about," I replied.

Scar stood up and moved from his seat. When he did, the aquarium came into better view. That gigantic one-eyed goldfish swam back and forth. Scar was testing me, so I focused on my feet instead.

"Don't know what I'm talking about?" Scar said. "Just how stupid do you think I am?"

"Mr. Scar, I mean no disrespect, but I don't know what you do. My family moved here a few weeks ago, my dad is a Colonel over at Gardner Army Base. I know I should know who you are, but I don't."

He twisted his lips. "Then let me explain it to you so there's no confusion. I'm Scar Pellano and I own the crime in this town. Wedge City is mine. I'm the crime boss and that means any crime happens in Wedge City, it's got to go through me. You didn't go through me and that's why we got a problem. And when we got a problem, it's up to me to find a solution." Scar danced his fingers along the table, just above where that trap door button was. "Okay, I think I got a solution. You want to score a load of peanut butter so bad? I'll give you a chance to prove yourself."

Scar must have gotten confused.

"But that's not it at all. I don't want a chance to prove myself, I just want to go home and forget this ever happened."

Scar cracked the knuckles on his right hand. "Don't test my patience, kid. You got two options." He pointed to my feet, actually to the red 'x' below my feet. "You can take door number one as they say," he looked sideways at one of his guys who smiled back at him and laughed. "Or you can choose the other option which is this: I give you three days to steal five hundred jars of peanut butter. You do that, then maybe I'll make room for you in my town."

"Room for me?"

"What are you deaf? Yes, you complete this job, then I'll give you permission to operate your own crew inside my town. You got a crew don't you?"

I shook my head.

"You gonna need a crew to steal five hundred jars of peanut butter, you know some people you trust?"

"I don't know anybody," I said.

Scar licked his lips, then looked down the table. "Hey, Sonny, you know anybody about this kid's age who might work with him?"

The man wiped his mouth. "Don't know boss, maybe Eddie?"

"Spaghetti Eddie?" roared Pellano. "I heard Kruger's got him chained down to detention the rest of the year." Scar stopped. "You know what, that could actually work. Hey, kid, you go get Spaghetti Eddie out of detention, I bet he'll work with you. Plus, he'll help you put together the kind of crew you need to pull of this job by Saturday night."

"But, I can't get this done by Saturday night!"

The room stopped. Forks screeched against plates. Scar glared at me, leaned over his plate. His finger danced over his scar then traveled downward until it finally slipped under the table.

Uh oh.

I stared down at that floor, wondering what on earth happened to people when they fell through the trap door.

Scar turned to know one in particular, hand still under the table. "Kids always scream real funny don't they?" He ran his finger along his zig-zag scar. "So long, Lenny."

"Okay, I'll do it!"

He straightened up and winked. "That's what I thought."

And that was it. Scar turned back to his meal, the men in the room continued their conversations, and the guard nodded for me to go. But I couldn't shake something.

"Um, Mr. Scar, sir?"

Scar turned back toward me, clearly annoyed.

"What is it kid?"

I swallowed hard. "I was just wondering, what happens, you know, when the floor opens up and everything?"

Scar looked around the room, then slapped his hand on the table so hard, his wine glass fell over and shattered. He busted out laughing and instantly the entire room lost it.

"You know, kid, you're funny. Now go put together a crew. You got three days to pull this job and give me fifty percent of your haul. Oh, and one more thing. You gotta steal this peanut butter without anyone finding out. I've made certain commitments. You screw this up and you're gonna find out exactly what happens when someone goes through my trap door."

CHAPTER NINE

I sat on the curb in front of Mr. Maple's food stand, my head hung between my knees, my breathing shallow and quick.

I was in trouble. Serious trouble. I replayed the entire episode in my head and tried to figure out how it had happened. I should tell the police, or my mom, or the Colonel.

My knees were shaking. I tried to stop them with my hands, but they were shaking too.

No way. I couldn't tell the police, or my mom, and definitely not the Colonel. I had somehow gotten myself into this mess, and I needed to find a way out.

Scar said I should start with Spaghetti Eddie. In addition to being curious about him, I was now also terrified of Eddie. If I was going to get his help doing anything, I couldn't do it alone. Eddie and his boot made it pretty clear what he'd do to me if I came near him again. There was only one person at McMillan who might, just might, help me. The only person who'd even talked to me.

Mega Bits.

Problem was, after what I'd said to her, I was quite certain she didn't want to speak to me again.

I found her the next day in the hall between second and third periods. She spit a piece of gum in my hair. Later at lunch, I went up to her table and she pulled lettuce out of her sandwich and threw it at me.

I got the hint and got depressed. I had only three days to get Eddie's help and steal me a load of peanut butter or I would get a close encounter with Scar Pellano's trap door.

After school, I was unlocking my bike when I noticed Mega Bits and her ridiculous hair bouncing down the sidewalk away from school. I let her move a block ahead and then I followed. About six blocks of neighborhood streets later, she turned into a white two-story house and walked around back. I waited five minutes. Maybe away from her friends and outside of school, I might have better luck. Or, maybe she'd find something much worse to throw at me.

I rang the doorbell and heard a shuffling of feet followed by the opening of the door. An older woman, maybe early seventies, stood there. She wore an apron and wiped her hands down the front. She smiled.

"Well hello there," she said. "Are you selling something today?"

"Um no, ma'am, I was wondering if I could talk to Mega Bits?"

"Megan?" The woman smiled. "She already went out back to the barn, I'm sure she wouldn't mind if you went over and knocked on the door." She held up a finger. "But wait." She shuffled back to the kitchen, then came back with a plate of chocolate-chip cookies. She handed them to me and smiled. "If you don't mind. This saves me a trip."

"Thank you, ma'am."

She gave a little wave and shut the door. I walked off the porch and around the house. There was a white, two-story barn behind the house. Beat up, worn off paint, with a metal rooster perched on the top.

I grabbed the brass door knob. "Owww!" I yelled while jumping back. Electric current traveled up my arm and shoulder.

A crackle came out of a speaker several feet above the door. I looked up. Next to the crackling was a small video camera.

"Unbelievable! You actually followed me home? I'm calling the police."

"No, Mega Bits, don't. Please." I held up the plate of cookies so she could see them.

"My grandmother's cookies?"

"Listen," I said while shaking my arm back to life. "I wanted to apologize for what I said."

"So you stalked me to my house to tell me you're sorry?"

"I was afraid of what you might throw at me if I tried to speak with you at school again."

"So invading my home was your best alternative?"

"Are you going to let me in?" I said.

The speaker crackled for several seconds. "I suppose you have taken my chocolate-chip cookies hostage."

Five seconds later, the door opened and Mega Bits stood there, glaring at me. Then, she grabbed the plate of cookies and shoved one in her mouth.

"Well," she said over a mouthful of chocolate. "I'm waiting."

"Oh, the apology, right. That stuff I said, I didn't mean in."

"Yeah, you did," she said.

"No really, I was just being a jerk. I'm sorry."

"No, Lenny, here's the thing. When people say mean things, they do mean it. Maybe not all of it, but at least some of it. You know what things people don't mean? The nice things. You basically called me and my friends losers."

She was right. I couldn't really take that back. I watched as she chewed her cookie, then I nodded and turned around and began to walk away.

"Don't walk away," she said from behind.

I stopped and turned around. She waved her hands around in circles. "This whole dopey, gloomy, 'woe is me' thing you've got going has got to change. You said something mean, it hurt, I threw stuff at you, and now you've apologized. That's good enough for me. You might as well come in." She walked into her barn. I followed.

Not sure what I expected, but when I heard barn, I expected hay, some old pitchforks and a workbench: typical barn stuff. What I saw was what I imagined Santa's workshop would look like if it collided with an electronics store.

Loud ticking clocks hung from the rafters. Christmas lights and wires crisscrossed from one end of the barn to the other. I heard a *"choo-choo"* and watched a small toy train move around a track that circumnavigated the barn about eight feet off the ground. The train stopped just above us. A bit of steam came out of its engine while the train whistle sounded. A pile of twelve old antique looking TVs with wooden panels was stacked against one wall like a pyramid. Wires and antennas filled up another wall and in the middle of it all, a computer desk with five monitors and a large flat screen monitor suspended from the rafters of the ceiling.

I spun around taking everything in.

"This place is amazing, I can't believe it, did you do all this yourself?"

Mega Bits smiled, then began chewing the inside of her cheek like she was studying me.

"So, what do you want?"

"Why do you think I want something?"

She put her hands in the pockets of her overalls. "You may dress like a Hardy boy, but I'm not willing to assume you act like one yet. Fact is, people start acting nice when they want something." She cocked an eyebrow. "So, what is it?"

I took a breath. "I don't think you'll believe me?"

"Why?"

"Because I'm not sure I believe it myself."

She chewed on her lip. "Come see this." She walked to the other side of her barn and pulled down on a lever. A jar lowered down from the ceiling. She opened up the jar, then dipped a cup into a yellow canister and picked up a cup of sugar. She dumped the sugar into jar, then hit the lever up and the jar rose to the ceiling.

"Just watch," she said while pointing up.

So I watched. The bowl was set onto a conveyor belt, which moved the bowl slowly to its next stop. I watched as, incredibly, every few feet, something different was done. First, butter was added, then eggs were cracked, then flour added, along with baking soda, Mega Bits pointed out. Then a mixer was placed into the mixture and a minute later the bowl was greeted by a cup of chocolate chips.

Mega Bits and I were following it now that the bowl had made it to the other side of the barn. The bowl tipped over and ran down a tube and then from there was squirted into small circles on a cookie sheet. From there, the pan went down another conveyor belt and stopped, just inches from Mega Bits. She picked it up.

"There, perfect chocolate chip cookies, now all we need is Granny to bake them."

"That—that was unbelievable."

She smiled. "I know. So trust me when I tell you, I'm accustomed to the unbelievable. But first, go take this pan to Granny, I have a feeling we're gonna need the sugar."

CHAPTER TEN

Mega Bits dunked her cookie in milk, and took another bite. "So let me get this straight: you've got to steal five hundred jars of peanut butter by Saturday night or Scar Pellano is going to send you through his trap door?"

I held up my finger. "And, he stressed that nobody can figure out that I stole the peanut butter."

She sucked her chin back and took another bite. "Wow! That really is unbelievable."

"And, he said that for me to pull this off, I'm going to need a crew."

"He's right," Mega Bits said.

"How would you know?"

She shrugged. "I didn't always live with my granny. My dad and mom were a mess, both criminals. I learned from watching them. Ended up in juvie for six months."

"You've been in jail?"

"Relax, it's not contagious. When I got out, granny took me in and, well, I've stayed mostly out of trouble ever since. The point is, Scar's right. You need a crew. Did he have anybody in mind?"

"He said I should get Spaghetti Eddie to help."

"Good choice, Eddie could figure out how to pull a job like that."

"Problem is, I think Spaghetti Eddie hates me."

"Aww, Eddie's just grouchy with everybody," Bits said.

"No really, he put his boot on my chest and told me he'd hurt me if I ever came near him again."

She shrugged. "Or he hates you."

"So how am I going to get him to help me?"

Bits finished chewing another cookie. "You're definitely going to need my help."

"You'll help me?"

She stood up and stretched. "It'll cost you."

"How much?" I said.

"I'll think about that, but you're running out of time and I bet I know how you can get Eddie to help you."

"How?"

"Have you seen him around school lately?"

"No."

"Because he's in detention. You find a way to get him out of detention, and I bet he'd help you."

"That's what Scar thought. Well, how hard can it be to get somebody out of detention?" I said.

"Ha, that's funny, you apparently have never met Helmet Kruger." She walked over to her desk and turned on her computer. "Then it's time to show you."

"Is he mean?" I asked.

"Kruger? Worse than mean, more like diabolical. The man likes pain. Likes seeing students in pain even more."

She was typing away at her keyboard.

"In the old days, the detention room was held inside of Kruger's office. Kruger would sit and work all day, only getting up to put the fear of God into his detainees. The only way out of that office was to go past his desk. If that wasn't bad enough, he had a big German shepherd named Boris that watched the students for him. Then about five years ago, they did some renovations and built a separate room connected to his office. Kruger brags that he's got the best detention facility in the state. I think I can find us the building plans online."

With a few clicks of her computer, she was on the County Planning website. "Okay, McMillan Junior High Detention ... right here." She clicked on it and building blueprints popped up on the large flat screen monitor hanging from the rafters. She pointed up.

"Okay, we've got a construction diagram of the room when it was added on five years ago, several pages of blueprints, even a story on Helmet Kruger himself."

She bounced up from her chair and walked up to the monitor. "Based on these construction documents, there are bars on the only window out and the only door is connected to Kruger's office. And like I said, that German shepherd will be guarding that exit at all times.

My heart sunk. "Then breaking someone out is impossible."

Mega Bits squinted, then jabbed a finger at the diagram. "Wait a second, what's this?"

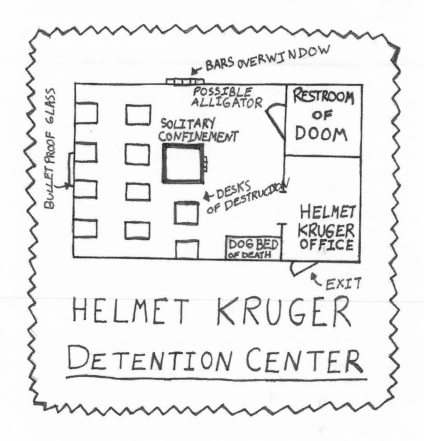

I looked too. It was a small square in the middle of the detention room. It was labeled Solitary Confinement. She put her hand on the monitor and swiped and the next page of blueprints popped up. It was the specs on a Solitary Confinement booth, like an overgrown phone booth with a single opening covered in steel bars.

Mega Bits gave me a look. "Like I said, Helmet Kruger likes to see students in pain."

"So I need to break a kid named Spaghetti Eddie out of Kruger's detention room, a room that looks almost impossible to get into. And Spaghetti Eddie may or may not be in the solitary confinement booth," I said.

"Eddie gets into more trouble than any other kid in that school," said Mega Bits. "I'd bet dollars to doughnuts that he's the kid you'll find in solitary confinement."

"Then that makes it even tougher," I said.

"Maybe...." Then her eyes sparkled, like she had an idea. "Or maybe not." Mega Bits started swiping through the rest of the blueprints, tracing her fingers along the diagrams.

"Granny's youngest son Nick runs a heating and air company. Sometimes I have to work with him so I've learned to read schematic diagrams. Right there, yep see." She pointed to something on the diagram and it didn't mean anything to me.

She rolled her eyes. "This is an air conditioning duct. Runs all the way under the detention room, from the looks of it, right under the center of the room. Right where the—"

"Solitary confinement booth sits," I said.

She patted me on the shoulder like I'd gotten a question right. "Yes, if you could get into that vent, you could cut through the bottom of the solitary confinement booth and break Spaghetti Eddie out of there."

"That's the craziest thing I've ever heard of, there's no way that would work."

She took her glasses and chewed on the end of them. Then she opened up a pack of grape Big League Chew and popped a handful into her mouth. She chomped down on the gum as she seemed to consider the problem. "Well then, we'll just have to poison Kruger *and* his dog."

She looked at me and held up her hands. "Not kill them mind you, just make them go to sleep for a while."

"I'm not exactly comfortable with poisoning," I said.

"Okay, you could attach industrial smoke bombs to rocks and throw them through the windows. Bars can't keep smoke out and then Kruger would be forced to let all the kids out." She rubbed her chin. "At least I think he'd let the kids out."

"Again," I said, "I'm afraid that the whole terrorism feel of it would put me in jail for the rest of my life."

"Then I think the vent is your only way in," Bits said.

"But how would I even get into the vent?"

She smiled, then dragged her finger along the diagram of the vent until it reached the outside wall.

"You really think it will work?" I asked.

She shrugged. "If we plan it right? Sure."

"And you'll really help me?"

She winked. "Like I said, it'll cost you."

CHAPTER ELEVEN

Bits hacked into the school's attendance program the next morning and made sure that both of us would be absent because of illness. Then, at 9:15 am, Mega Bits and I stood across from McMillan Junior High waiting for our delivery. A white van with the words *AAA Heating and Air* pulled up to the curb and the driver's window rolled down.

A young man with a stubbly beard and a baseball cap appeared. He spoke while a cigarette dangled out of his mouth.

"You got the payment?" he asked.

I held up the white bag in my hands. The guy
looked both ways then, apparently satisfied nothing
weird was going on, opened up the side door to his
van.

"Get In."

Mega Bits and I jumped in and I handed the bag
up. He put his nose inside and took a big whiff. Then
he turned and smiled. "Mimi's truly has the best
donuts in the world. Like angels come in and blow
pure magic into these little fried rings of dough." He
stuffed a cherry donut in his mouth, cigarette still
dangling to one side. I'd never heard somewhat
speak so eloquently about donuts before and never
seen someone eat a donut and smoke a cigarette at
the same time.

The guy turned. "Hey, Megs."

"Hey, Uncle Nick," said Megan as she started
rifling through the contents of a black duffel bag.

"Got uniforms for you both right there.
Pullovers you can slip on. And you should have
everything you need in that bag. Screw drivers,

wrenches, duct tape, rope, and the smallest molten torch cutter I could find."

Mega Bits held it up so I could see it.

"Looks like a hot glue gun," I said.

Nick snorted from the front. "I assure you it's not. That baby will cut through a half an inch of sheet metal. Concrete too. Think of it as the light saber of the heating and air world. You got the building plans, Megs?"

"Sure do. Thanks again, Unc, we owe you."

"Are you kidding? Mimi's donuts *and* you're going to sneak one past ole' Helmet Kruger?" He shrugged. "That's good enough for me."

Bits and I us put our *AAA Heating & Air* coveralls over our other clothes and then slipped on our caps. Mega Bits grabbed the black bag and we jumped out of the van. She slid the door shut, then rapped on the door. Nick grinned with a big donut stuck between his teeth and the cigarette still stuck in the corner of his mouth.

We carried the equipment over the school's lawn past some trees, behind the bushes and slid up against the detention room and its cement block wall. Bits crawled around the foundation until she stopped.

"This is it, right here."

We knelt down, Mega Bits grabbed the electric screwdriver and started unscrewing metal screws from the vent. She took the vent cover off and flipped on her flashlight.

"It'll be a tight fit. Glad I'm not going down there." She handed me a walkie-talkie and a tape measure then tied a rope to the end of my foot."

"Last chance Lenny. Sure you want to do this?"

"Definitely not sure. But I *am* sure I don't want to visit Scar's trap door."

I grabbed the end of the tape measure, pushed the duffel bag in front of me and took a few deep breaths. The walkie-talkie was hooked to my collar and turned down low so I didn't make too much noise. Megan's voice crackle through. "Testing one, two, three."

"Roger," I replied.

I squeezed into the tube, started pushing the duffel bag, tape measure in left hand, small flashlight in my right hand. I inched my way down the tube while Bits updated me via the walkie-talkie.

"You're at fourteen feet now. Go another foot and a half and you should be at the spot. How are you feeling?"

"Like I'm stuck in a tube under the ground."

"Fair enough. Okay, few more inches. Just. About. There. Stop. The Solitary Confinement booth should be directly overhead. You ready with the molten torch? Remember, unless you want to come out of there looking like a piece of Swiss cheese, do not aim it at yourself."

I took the mini torch out of my tool belt, turned it on, and adjusted the power level. I waited a minute while it warmed up and I envisioned the circle I would cut out of the top of the vent. I turned to my back.

"You've got the goggles on, right?" said Bits. "You don't want bits of metal and cement falling into your eyes."

I found the goggles on the work belt and put them on.

"Goggles on now."

"What a rookie," Bits said. "Okay, take it slow. You'll have to cut through the vent first, then the floor. Lenny, you do know that what you're doing is completely nuts, right?"

"What if we're wrong and I end up cutting a hole right in the middle of the classroom floor, what are we going to do?"

"You're gonna lie through your teeth and I'm gonna run."

"That's real comforting," I said.

I pulled the trigger to the torch, a skinny green flame poured out, and stopped two inches from the end of the torch. I could feel the heat. I moved it to the edge of the vent and slowly started to cut out a circle. A minute later, the circle started bending in, like a can of vegetables does when using a can opener. I cut the last little bit and the metal circle fell on my face.

"Okay, I'm through the vent," I said rubbing my nose. I shined my flashlight on the space above me. "The floor is made up of wooden rafters, with plywood on top of it, just like you said. The solitary confinement booth is probably built on top of that."

"Okay," Bits said. "This will probably take a few passes. On the first, you'll take out the rafters. On the second path, the plywood subfloor, and on your final pass, you should be able to break through the solitary confinement booth. Adjust the torch to maximum power."

I turned the knob and the green molten torch grew to four inches.

I once again started working in a circular arc, moving the torch slowly, amazed as it cut through the wood like a hot knife through soft butter. The rafters came off with ease. So did the plywood. I knocked softly and could tell the booth was definitely made out of metal. I picked a spot in the middle and used my torch to make a small quarter-sized hole.

I saw light and heard a shuffling above me.

"Spaghetti Eddie," I whispered. "Is that you?"

More shuffling above me, then an eyeball appeared.

"What are you doing?" said a low growl belonging to that single eye.

"I'm getting you out of here," I explained. "Now stand to edge of the booth while I cut a larger hole in the floor."

The eyeball stayed in the hole for another five seconds, like it was taking a measure of me. Then finally it was gone.

I made my final pass with the torch, keeping my free hand on the middle of the metal circle so it didn't land on my face. Finally, I'd made it through, lowered the metal piece through to the vent and put it off to the side.

Now the face attached to that voice was staring at me in the middle of the circle. And something was wrong.

"You're that idiot kid who was following me?"

"Yeah," I whispered back.

"This might be one of the creepier stalker moves in history."

I felt my face get warm and I started to stammer. "I-I just need to get you out of here."

"Says who?"

I didn't have time to explain everything to him. Not here, not now. So I said the only thing I thought would get him to move.

"Scar Pellano, that's who."

His eyes grew big.

"Scar sent you?"

"Yeah, so can we get out of here now?"

He shook his head. "When Kruger finds me missing at the end of the day, he'll give me double detention. No thanks."

"I thought of that. Just a second."

I grabbed the duffle bag and pushed it through the hole and up to Eddie.

"What's this?"

"Inside, you'll see."

He unzipped the duffel.

"A stuffed animal?"

"It's Cocoa, my bear, and the largest stuffed animal I own. Dress it up in your clothes, set it in your chair, then you come back before the end of the day. You'll find a heating and air uniform in there too. Put it on."

He hesitated a moment and then his face hardened and he grabbed Cocoa and the disguise.

I watched through the hole as Eddie put his clothes on Cocoa and then put the heating and air uniform on.

He slipped down through the hole and into the vent. I handed him the roll of duct tape and then held the metal circle from the bottom of the solitary confinement booth. "Duct tape it back in place." He did that, then I notified Mega Bits via the walkie-talkie that we were ready to leave.

Bits tugged the rope on my foot and I started to crawl backwards slowly. Spaghetti Eddie followed me. Five minutes later, we made it to the outside vent. I came out first, followed by Eddie.

He looked surprised when he saw Mega Bits. "You're involved in this too?"

"Yeah," she said as she peaked over the bushes.

The three of us rose up from the bushes, kept our heads down and walked quickly away from the school. Once we'd crossed the street, we kept walking until we reached a set of bushes where Mega Bits slipped inside. She started pulling off her coveralls and we followed.

She collected our uniforms and placed them in a plastic bag.

"Okay then," Spaghetti Eddie finally said. "You gonna tell me what this is all about?"

"Peanut butter," I finally said. "This is all about peanut butter."

CHAPTER TWELVE

Spaghetti Eddie had pulled a large magnifying glass out of his trench coat and was examining me. "So let me get this straight, the way I feel about spaghetti is the way you feel about peanut butter?"

I nodded.

"And somehow, Scar Pellano thinks you want to be a criminal and so he's giving you a test."

"It all happened so fast, but yes, I think that's the gist of it."

"And you need to steal five hundred jars of peanut butter by Saturday night or else," Eddie slid his finger across his throat.

I swallowed, then nodded slowly.

Eddie put the magnifying glass back inside his trench coat and paced back and forth. He finally stopped and took a deep breath. He reached back into his trench coat and pulled out a skateboard, dropped it on the ground and hopped on.

"I need to eat. Try to keep up."

Eddie took off down the sidewalk and Bits and I ran after him. Three exhausting blocks later, he skidded to a stop, flipped up his board and opened the door to Big Dawg Burgers.

Bits and I followed him in and when the burger and French fry smells hit my nose, my stomach did cartwheels. And not in a good way.

Eddie could see the concern on my face.

"Listen, Lenny. We can't do this if we're hungry. Until we get peanut butter back, you have to find other food to eat. Big Dawg Burgers are a nice runner-up. You'll see."

Mega Bits scrunched her face. "But if you like pasta so much, why aren't we at a spaghetti joint?"

"I usually try to avoid Pellano's and the other Italian joint is closed today."

Avoiding Pellano's made sense to me. As we walked in, a bell rang and the cooks behind the counter yelled, "Spaghetti Eddie!"

Eddie gave them a thumbs up, then led us to a corner booth. He plopped down and a nice waitress hustled over with a large pitcher of root beer and three glasses.

Eddie poured three glasses, then took a long, slow sip. He wiped the foam from his mouth with the back of his hand.

"So you think you love peanut butter as much as I like spaghetti, eh?"

"Probably more," I said while taking a long, slow sip from my own mug.

Eddie pulled out a nickel, set it up on the table with one hand and flicked it with the other. The nickel spun like a top, while both of us watched it. Finally, Eddie slapped the nickel down with his palm. He looked up at me and squinted.

"When was peanut butter invented?"

For a second, I thought he was joking. But he didn't blink. He was testing me. I licked my lips.

"Most people think it was George Washington Carver."

Eddie tilted his head and raised his eyebrows.

"But it wasn't," I explained. "Aztec Indians had been doing it for centuries when the patent for commercially making peanut butter was issued to Marcellus Edson."

"You could have just made that up," said Eddie.

"I'm a terrible liar," I responded.

He scratched his neck. "Okay, just wanted to make sure you're legit."

Mega Bits rolled her eyes. "And breaking a total stranger out of detention didn't prove that," she said.

"Fair enough," said Eddie. "So, those weird blue suit guys took all the peanut butter. That much I know. You two know anything else?"

I shook my head. "No. Scar said I needed to pull this job and I should get your help. Since the last conversation we had, I was on the ground and you had your boot on my chest, I figured I needed some assistance in convincing you. So I asked Mega Bits to help me."

The waitress came back with the largest burger I'd ever seen in my life.

"Your friends here want one?"

Eddie shook his head. "They'll share with me."

She left.

"We will?" Bits and I said together.

Eddie sunk his knife into the burger and cut it up three ways. Then he pointed the knife at me. "Like I said, Lenny, you gotta start eating more food. You don't need to like it, but you gotta eat. If I learned to do it, so can you."

He reached his hand into his trench coat and pulled out some metal contraption. It had a hand crank on the side. He dropped his burger into the machine and started to crank the handle. After

Eddie had cranked the handle several times, something started to ooze out of the side. I watched in fascination as long, skinny little strings started to fall out of the machine.

And then I realized what he was doing.

He was turning that hamburger into ... spaghetti.

At some point, the stuff stopped oozing onto the plate, and he set his contraption to the side and smiled at me. "Bet you've never seen someone turn a hamburger into spaghetti before, have you?"

He reached into his coat and pulled out a red bottle. He opened the cap, and when he did, I could smell the familiar aroma of spaghetti sauce. He shook it around then started to pour it all over his pile of Big Dawg Burger spaghetti. Finally, he grabbed his fork, twirled his freshly pressed noodles together and took a gigantic bite.

"You want to try it?" he said, holding a forkful of this strange food across the table.

My stomach did sommersaults and what little food I had eaten that morning felt like it wanted to come back up. I pushed past Mega Bits and ran to the bathroom. A few minutes later, my stomach settled down, and I walked back to our booth, my face flush from embarrassment.

"Lenny, you may have this weird stalker vibe going for you, but I appreciate you getting me out of detention, I really do." He pointed his fork at me this time. "But if I'm gonna help you pull this job, you gotta have your wits about you. You need to eat. So, here's the deal." He pushed a third of the burger in my direction. "You either try it or I'll put an ad in the newspaper saying you're scared of girls and sleep with a big pink teddy bear every night."

"But I'm not afraid of girls and I don't sleep—"

"And that embarrassing tattoo of Justin Bieber next to your bellybutton." He pointed at my belly.

"Wait a second—"

Eddie waved his hand in front of his face. "Or I can walk outta here right now and go back to detention and let Scar's trap door swallow you whole. Your choice."

I stared down at that burger and I loosened my collar.

"And, Lenny," Eddie continued. "Once we get your peanut butter back, you can renew your obsession. For now, you've got to eat other food."

Mega Bits bumped me with her shoulder. "You got this, Lenny."

I picked up the burger, closed my eyes, and brought it to my mouth. I bit off a corner and immediately tried to drown it with root beer. I swallowed as quickly as I could.

Mega Bits nudged me again. "Good?"

"I didn't throw up," I said.

"Okay, Lenny," said Eddie. "You keep eating and I'll start talking. To pull off a job like this, Scar is right, you need a crew. Mega Bits, you're good with computers, right?"

"Computers, electronics, anything like that," Bits said.

"Good, so you can handle the technical side of things. That leaves us in need of a chameleon and a driver."

"A chameleon?" I asked while contemplating my next bite. I had to admit, although I hated the grizzly texture of the burger, my stomach hadn't once wretched. I took another sip of root beer.

"A master of disguise," Eddie said while twisting his burger spaghetti around his fork and piling it into his mouth. "And I think I know where to find us one." He took two more bites, watched me take two more bites, then hollered up to the waitress.

"Put it on my tab, Flo!"

She snapped her towel from across the restaurant. "No problem, you little animal. See you next week."

We left Big Dawg's and Eddie jumped onto his board and sailed down Main Street. Four exhausting blocks later, we found ourselves in front of The Roy G Biv Community Theatre. I looked up at the sign, then turned to Spaghetti Eddie.

"Shakespeare?" I asked.

He smiled. "Just trust me."

CHAPTER THIRTEEN

Spaghetti Eddie led us to the back of the community playhouse where we watched dress rehearsal of a play called The Merchant of Venice. The play was about a young guy named Bassonio who likes a girl and needs money to visit her so he makes his best friend Antonio ask a mean old guy named Shylock for the money. Antonio is such a good friend, he promises to let Shylock cut a pound of flesh from his body if he fails to pay Bassonio's debt.

If you're thinking that's really messed up, then you're right. And it was awesome, in a really creepy couldn't take my eyes away sort of thing. And this was only the dress rehearsal. At the end, Eddie turned to Bits and I. "The best actor in the play, that's the next member of your crew."

"Who's that?" I asked.

"Who do you think?"

"Well, the old guy playing Shylock was the best, but I thought we were coming to find another kid?"

Spaghetti Eddie smiled. "Come on, let's go backstage." We followed Eddie and we weaved our way through the cast, when we saw the man who played Antonio hugging the short old guy who played Shylock.

After hugging, Shylock turned, saw us and cocked his head. "You're not in the play," he said in his gruff voice.

"Is it safe to talk here?" asked Eddie.

Shylock froze, his eyes twitched uncomfortably, then he flipped over a chair in front of us and sprinted away.

"Crap," Spaghetti Eddie said while jumping over the upside down chair. "We've got a runner!" Eddie plopped onto his board and gave chase.

I looked at Mega Bits. "Why is Eddie chasing after Shylock?"

She shrugged. "Beats me, but it looks like fun, come on, Lenny." Mega Bits sprinted away and I reluctantly followed.

Mega Bits and I were weaving through the theatre and ran through an open door under an exit sign. Eddie was weaving his skateboard through oncoming traffic, making his way towards a sprinting Shylock who was heading into Wedge City's bustling shopping district.

Bits and I sprinted across the street, and caught up to Eddie at the corner. He was pointed to his right.

"I lost him in Ruffalo's."

"The fancy woman's clothing store?" Bits asked.

Eddie nodded and motioned with his hand. "Keep your eyes open for anything strange."

We walked into Ruffalo's, and a tall woman with red hair and a rather severe expression stared at us. "May I help you?" she said through puckered lips.

Mega Bits stepped up. "Just looking for a birthday gift for our aunt."

"Oooh," the woman said while adjusting her glasses. Then she saw a woman waving to her from the dressing room and gave us one last stare before walking away.

"Okay," Spaghetti Eddie said. "Search every nook and cranny."

"Excuse me," a voice said from behind us. "Are you by chance looking for someone?"

"Yes," I said.

The woman was short with blonde hair pulled back in a ponytail. Her name tag said Kimberly. She pointed down the hall toward the back. "A very strange old man ran down the hall and out the back."

"Out the back?" Eddie said.

Kimberly nodded and jabbed her finger into the air. "Yep, you might want to hurry if you hope to catch him."

Eddie dropped his skateboard in the middle of the store, hopped on and was off, Mega Bits and I following close behind. Eddie was at the end in no time, pushing the exit door out, when an image flashed in my head, of Kimberly pointing towards the back. With old creaky hands that had hair coming out the knuckles and looked like they wouldn't belong to a Kimberly. They would belong to a—?"

I stopped. "An old man. Guys, we've been tricked. Come on." I ran back to the front of the store to find a pile of clothes in a heap along with a name tag that read *Kimberly*.

"Kimberly was Shylock!" Bits said in astonishment.

We hustled out the door and looked both ways. Shoppers filled up both sidewalks and if Shylock was among them, we had no idea where to begin.

"We lost him," Eddie growled.

Eddie was right. We had.

"And now you see why the Chameleon is so valuable," he said as we walked away.

"Do you have any other people in mind?" Bits asked.

Eddie shook his head. "Nobody this good." We walked in silence down to the end of the block when someone punched me in the back of the shoulder. "Hey you," a high pitched voice said from behind me.

I turned around. It was a short girl, about my age, with short black hair and light brown skin. Japanese American was my guess based off my time living in Okinawa when I was little.

"What do you creeps want anyway?" she asked.

Eddie stepped up. "Two Faced Tina I presume?"

She folded her arms and twisted her mouth. "Tina Miaki, but yeah that's what some people call me."

"Why'd you run from us?" Eddie asked.

Tina stepped closer. "Cuz I had to be certain you weren't trouble."

"And are you certain now?" said Eddie.

"I'm willing to listen to whatever you got to say," Tina said.

"Wait a second," I said, still trying to understand what was happening. "You, you were Shylock?"

"Yeah," Tina said. "What of it?"

"Well, you were incredible!" I said.

Her face relaxed, but only a little.

"And then you turned into Kimberly at the store?" Bits asked.

Two Faced Tina nodded.

I pointed at her. "But you must have forgotten to take off your hairy Shylock hands."

She let out a low growl. "I thought somebody might have caught that." She looked at Eddie, up and down. "You must be Spaghetti Eddie."

"How'd you know?" Eddie asked.

"Mohawk and a trench coat. Not exactly traveling incognito. So stop wasting my time and tell me what this is all about."

Eddie ran his hand over his Mohawk. "Listen, Lenny here has a job, and he needs the best

Chameleon around. I told him I heard you were the best."

She glared at Eddie while folding her arms. Then she looked at me. "And I heard the great Spaghetti Eddie works alone. Now you're putting together a crew? Must be quite a job."

Spaghetti Eddie pulled me forward. "First of all, it's Lenny here who's pulling together the crew and yeah, it's a big job *and* time sensitive."

She put a finger to her chin and spun around and started to walk away. Then she spun back around. "So Spaghetti Eddie, overall girl, and mystery man Lenny here want me for a job, a big job. I'll bite. Here's my price. I want to be Ebenezer Scrooge in this year's production of the Christmas Carol. That buffoon Elliot Turnbull has had the part the last ten years running and I think it's time for some new blood."

I looked at Eddie and he gave me a little nod.

With Scar Pellano on one side of the equation and doing favors for my crew on the other side, I really didn't have much of a choice. I had no idea how I would get her the part, but it sounded better than whatever was under that trap door.

"Ebenezer Scrooge?" I said. "Yeah, I can do that."

She practically stepped on my toes and glared up at me. "I'll expect you to keep your promise or I really will extract a pound of flesh from you just like Shylock."

I laughed but stopped when I realized she wasn't laughing, and quickly nodded my head.

She shot out her hand. "I've got two rules. One, I handle my part of the job the way I want to. No questions asked. Two, nobody's allowed to fall in love with me. When you're cursed with beauty and a sunny disposition, boys fall for you all the time. But I'm already involved. I have a long and tortured relationship with the theatre. I don't need any other distractions."

"I think I can manage that," said Eddie.

Two Faced Tina made a face. "We'll see."

"Okay, so just Lenny here is our fearless leader and Spaghetti Eddie can do it all. I've heard of an overalls girl who's some kind of computer genius. I assume that's you?"

Megan beamed with pride. "Name's Mega Bits."

Tina nodded. "Okay then, I'll handle all disguises and reconnaissance. If this really is a big job, then that leaves us looking for a driver." She turned to Eddie. "Who's on your list?"

Eddie took a crumpled up piece of paper out of his trench coat and showed it to Tina. She scanned it over, working from the top. "They're no good." She kept tracking her finger down the page. "They're good, but I wouldn't trust them. This last one, so-so. And if this is a big job, so-so won't do. You need great."

"You got a name?" Spaghetti Eddie asked.

"I got a phone number. Been holding off on using it until the time was right."

"The time is right," said Eddie.

Tina pulled out her cell and dialed a number. "Yeah, Two Faced Tina here. We need a driver. A job. Big Job. Yeah. At the mall? Got it. No, we won't be late."

She got off the phone. "He'll meet us outside the Pretzel Shoppe at 1:30pm."

CHAPTER FOURTEEN

An hour later, we sat, staring at the people coming in and out of the mall, trying to guess which one might be our next driver, when a giant security guard, with curly black hair, a large oval head, and light brown skin came towards us. He folded his arms and started to speak.

I'm not exactly sure what I expected to come out of his mouth, but not a high pitched voice traveling as quickly as a bullet train. Kinda like the sound speedy Gonzalez might make if he was dropped off a cliff.

I looked at the others and they shrugged.

Tina took the lead. "Hey, pal, could you say that again but this time slower?"

He slowed it down alright, but I was only able to make out a few of the words.

Tina turned and frowned. "He needs us to follow him outside."

Spaghetti Eddie protested as I'm sure he often did in the face of law enforcement. "Leave us alone dude, we're not doing anything wrong."

But big scary, Speedy Gonzalez talking security guard wasn't listening. He was walking, and walking rather wobbly, towards the exit doors. His hand tapping away at his Billy club. Something about this guy wasn't quite right and I didn't want to make him mad. So I started to follow and the others came too.

We got outside and he kept walking, towards the dumpster. Now this didn't feel right at all. But then, the weirdest thing happened.

The security guard broke into two pieces. Literally. I was ten feet behind him, staring at him when his upper half jumped down from his lower half.

And then where I half expected blood to start gushing from his lower half, instead a head popped up. A head that looked remarkably like the head on the big security guard. Oval, tan, with curly black hair.

I turned to Mega Bits. She looked equally mystified.

The two curly black-haired halves of the original giant security guard ran behind the dumpster and came back a minute later.

Both were dressed in black athletic shorts. The one on the left wore a black football jersey with the number forty-three and the one on the right wore a yellow jersey with the number forty-three. Each wore a yellow headband.

The one wearing the black shirt started to talk, just like the big security guard did. The words came out so quickly I couldn't catch up.

"Hey," Tina yelled. "SLOW. IT. DOWN!"

"Pardon me, Mademoiselle. I tend to get excited, well, about everything. I am Al Salamua and this is my twin brother Sal. People call me Annoying Al and people call him Silent Sal. We're the best driver you've ever seen and you said you're looking for the best."

Tina must have heard the same thing I did because her face wrinkled into confusion. "Did you say you and your brother are the best driver, don't you mean best drivers?"

"As you can see Mademoiselle Tina, my brother and I were not gifted with great height. But what we lack in femur length, we make up for in talent. Although we both can drive, we are at our best working as a team. I steer, he pushes the pedals, but let me assure you. You'll not find a better driver than us."

Two short kids driving as one person? That was the craziest thing I'd ever heard and I was beginning to wonder why Tina thought this was a good idea. She turned and gave us a weird look. Looks like she might agree with me.

"Annoying Al, could you give us a moment?" asked Spaghetti Eddie.

We all huddled together and Tina was the first to speak. "Sorry, guys, my contact never told me it was a couple of short kids."

Spaghetti Eddie was next. "Yeah, this must be some kind of joke, no way they can drive us." Eddie looked at me. "Lenny, you'll need to let them know."

"Me?"

"It's your crew."

"Yeah, well, I guess it is."

I turned towards Al and Sal. Al stood with his hands behind his back smiling, Sal stood with his arms folded scowling. They were waiting.

"Um, Mr. Al?" I said.

He raised up on his tippy toes. "She's Two Faced Tina and we assume the other one is Spaghetti Eddie. That makes overalls there the computer girl. Who are you?" He asked.

"I'm Lenny."

"Lenny what?" he asked.

"Just Lenny and this is, um, my crew." Being twelve and all, I'd never fired somebody before, and even though I didn't want these guys driving a car for us, they were cute and cuddly in a large teddy bear sort of way, and I didn't want to hurt their feelings. Then I thought of the Colonel. The Colonel wouldn't care about hurting their feelings.

"The thing is, we were expecting somebody, well, different to be our driver. I'm afraid this isn't going to work for us."

Al's face fell immediately, and suddenly he looked just like Sal.

"But we really appreciate the meeting," I added quickly. "So, um, best of luck to you." I turned around.

"You were expecting someone taller?" Al asked. I spun around and he didn't even have a trace of a smile.

"Excuse me?" I said.

"You were expecting someone taller, no?"

"Well, maybe. Probably just a miscommunication. But thanks for meeting us anyway." Like an idiot, I waved. Then backed away as Al leaned into Sal and began talking to him in hushed whispers. Finally, Al stepped away while Sal took his shirt off.

"Excuse me, Mr. Lenny?"

"Yes?"

"My brother Sal has agreed to destroy you."

I looked at Mega Bits then back at Al. "Excuse me?"

"My brother and I discussed it. We are the greatest driver in the world and you have insulted our honor and the honor of all the great short drivers everywhere." Sal leaned in, grunted something and Al held his finger up. "And jockeys. You've insulted short drivers and jockeys. Thus, there is only one option left. Sal has decided to bring you a hurricane of pain in a duel of fists. I will now ready the ring of honor while you prepare yourself for an agonizing death. In our family, Sal is known to be meaner than a caged muskrat."

Sal started to punch the air like he was warming up for a boxing contest. I looked at Al, his face stone serious. These guys weren't kidding.

Eddie came up behind me and started rubbing my shoulders. "Okay, Lenny, I'm not sure you can take him but at least get a few shots in before, well, you know?"

"Before what?" I asked.

Tina ran a finger across her throat.

I shook Eddie off. "Wait a second, I'm not going to fight this kid. Please, Al, is there any other way you and your brother can reclaim your honor?"

Al once again put his hands behind his back as he gave me a long cold stare. "Allow us to prove we are the greatest driver in the world. Then our honor will be restored and Sal will not be forced to pummel you with his fists of death."

"Sounds fair to me."

"How do you want to prove it to us?" asked Mega Bits.

Al made a face. "Pick a car. Any car from the lot."

We looked upon the cars staggered through the mall's parking lot. Tina grew a mischievous smile and spoke up. "How about that cherry red Porsche out there in the middle of the lot?"

Al grabbed Tina's hand and kissed it. She shook it free and stepped back. "Oooh, gross!"

"Mademoiselle Tina, you are a woman of style."

"True, but I'm also twelve and far meaner than a caged muskrat so don't ever touch my hand again if you expect to keep breathing."

Al tilted his head. "As you wish, my lady. I invite you and your friends to watch our dazzling display of death defying driving."

Al bowed, then he and Sal walked towards the red Porsche when all of a sudden, the boy made a sharp right and started running. We watched as they ran across the parking lot towards a black and yellow van with the number forty-three on the side. The two wild haired kids hopped in the driver side. A moment later, the van roared to life, pulled out of its spot, and took off in a direction opposite from the Porsche. But only for a few seconds. Then the van made a sharp turn, and its engine rumbled. It rumbled some more. Then, the tires screeched, smoke kicked up from behind, and the van shot across the pavement.

I suddenly had a very bad feeling about this. They were heading directly toward the cherry red Porsche.

"What are they doing?" I asked out loud.

The van picked up speed. No doubt about it, they were headed straight for the Porsche. Not moving away at all.

Oh my goblets, they were going to ram the car. I had insulted the wrong crazy guys. The impact would be terrible. I wanted to look away, but I couldn't. And then suddenly, the most improbable thing happened.

Just before the van smashed the Porsche, it jerked hard to the left, screeched to a stop for a moment before the van's momentum flipped it over and high into the air. The van tumbled over through the air, flying over the cherry red Porsche, then, incredibly, landed on the other side of the Porsche not ever touching it once. The van just rocked back and forth a few times, exhaust coming out of its back tailpipe until, the van finally turned off and Annoying Al and Silent Sal jumped out.

The two brothers ran into each other, jumped, and bumped chests. They had just sideways flipped a van over a seventy-thousand dollar sports car. It was the craziest thing I'd ever seen in my life.

I looked at Spaghetti Eddie whose mouth was open in astonishment. "I think we just found a new driver," he said.

"Or two," I said.

CHAPTER FIFTEEN

Mega Bits and I helped Spaghetti Eddie sneak back into detention before the end of school. Twenty minutes later, the bell rang and Eddie came out of school riding his skateboard with a satisfied smile.

"Kruger never suspected a thing," he said.

We met Silent Sal, Annoying Al, and Two Faced Tina at Megan's barn.

"So let me get this straight," Tina said while sniffing one of granny's chocolate chip cookies. "Scar Pellano wants you to steal five hundred jars of peanut butter, or else he's going to send you down the hole in his floor?"

"Yes," I said.

"And we know the peanut butter's been taken by a bunch of guys wearing blue suits and wearing silver glasses?" she asked.

"But driving green vans," said Eddie as he dumped a handful of chocolate chip cookies into his pasta machine and began to turn the crank.

"Any idea where the peanut butter's been taken?" Tina asked

Mega Bits spun around in her computer chair. "Last night, I was able to hack into the city's traffic cameras and gather the footage from the previous week. I wrote a program that scanned the footage for green cargo vans. I was able to detect a convergence of green vans towards the northwest edge of town at the intersection of Highways 50 and 6."

"Is there a big warehouse in that part of town?" asked Spaghetti Eddie as he squirted spaghetti sauce onto his chocolate chip cookie noodles.

Mega Bits shook her head. "Don't think so. The vans appear to head out of town."

"Any idea where they're headed?" I asked.

Mega Bits smiled and hit a couple of buttons on her computer and an overhead satellite image popped up on the large flat screen monitor hanging down from the rafters. "My guess is right here. Five miles outside of town. The National Science Research Lab."

Eddie scratched his chin while crumbly chocolate chip noodles fell from his chin. "Makes sense. Peanut Butter has a defect, the government declares it unsafe, so they take it to a research lab to have it tested." He looked up. "So, we've got to break into the National Science Research Lab?"

Mega Bits shook her head. "I don't think we need to." She pulled up more images. "Over the last three days, vans have continued to trickle into town and head back out. I'd bet anything they're picking up the last remnants of the peanut butter and taking it to the Research Lab."

Tina pointed at Bits. "You think a van holds enough peanut butter don't you?"

Bits nodded. "If I had to guess, yes, a van fully loaded probably carries five hundred jars of peanut butter. And what's better, I can track those vans once they come into town."

Tina stepped closer to the flat screen. "Show us."

Mega Bits cracked her knuckles. She punched a couple of buttons and the screen split into two. On the left hand side was a live feed of the intersection at 50 and 6. On the right were dozens of different black and white still photos. "Two days ago, eighteen vans came into Wedge City, picked up loads at various points around the city and then left the city, presumably to go to the Research Center. One day ago, only eight vans came into Wedge City."

"What's that mean?" I asked.

"My guess is we're running out of time," said Eddie.

"How about today, how many vans?" I asked.

"Since I was gone all day, I haven't checked yet. Just a second." She hit a couple buttons and danced her fingers across her desk. "Okay, looks like a grand total of ... wait a second, that can't be right." Her head popped up, full of concern.

"How many?" I asked.

"None," she said.

I jumped up. "None?"

"Yeah, I'm really sorry, Lenny. Not one."

"I think you're wrong," said Two Faced Tina. "This shot on the left is a live feed right?"

"Yeah, why?" said Mega Bits.

Tina stepped aside and pointed. "Isn't this a green van waiting at the intersection of 50 and 6?"

Bits hit a button and zoomed in on the image.

"Two Faced Tina's right. Green van, heading into the city now. If the pattern's consistent, it will take them anywhere from ten to fifteen minutes to reach their destination, twenty to thirty minutes to load up, and another ten to fifteen minutes before they make it back to the edge of town. In total, about an hour."

"And the fact that it's the only van today?" Eddie asked.

"My guess," said Bits while taking a deep breath. "It's probably also the last van."

Tina raised her finger. "Which means if Lenny's going to get his peanut butter back, it needs to be now."

Spaghetti Eddie wiped sauce off his mouth and stuck his pasta maker back into his trench coat. "Okay, Mega Bits, you track the van for us. Al and Sal will drive; Tina, you come up with a disguise to distract the driver, then Lenny and I will go in hard and fast. Simple smash and grab, they won't know what hit them."

I cleared my throat and stood up. "I don't think that will work."

Eddie looked annoyed. "Why?"

"Well, because Scar made it clear I had to steal it in such a way that nobody would know it was missing. He said he's got some kind of deal he has to protect."

Spaghetti Eddie blew air out through his lips. "Well that makes things more difficult."

"How much?" I asked.

Tina frowned. "About a thousand percent."

"Clock's ticking guys," Bits said from her computer. "fifty-seven minutes or so."

Eddie ran his hand over his Mohawk, and paced in front of the flat screen. Finally, he spun around and waved his finger at Tina.

"Okay, then we find another way. What if we tried to pull a Lazy Bucket?"

Tina folded her arms and squinted. "You mean a Lazy Bucket with a Donald Trump?"

"It could work?" Eddie said, not so sure.

"No, it can't. To pull it off right, we'd need a tiger, and no way can we get our hands on a tiger in the next fifty-seven minutes."

"Fifty-six minutes," Mega Bits yelled out.

"Okay," Eddie continued, "how about a Dimpled Susan?"

It was like they were speaking a foreign language.

"Straight up?" asked Annoying Al who had now come in from outside and joined the conversation.

"Why not?" said Eddie.

"Wouldn't we need more people to pull off a Dimpled Susan?" said Al.

Eddie shrugged. I felt like they had all read very different nursery rhymes than I.

The barn grew quiet again. Awkwardly quiet.

Tina stomped her foot and punched Eddie in the shoulder.

"I've got it. This situation calls for a Ponderosa Shake."

Eddie slapped his palm onto his forehead. "That's brilliant, why hadn't I thought of that?"

"Because," Tina said, "you are a boy and boys are morons."

A broad smile grew across Eddie's face. "But not just a Ponderosa Shake, one with a Texas Twist?"

"Exactly," said Tina stepping towards him. "And just a hint of Louisiana Shuffle."

"Whoa," said Eddie, stepping backwards, like he'd just been given the answer to the meaning of life.

Al stepped towards Tina, grabbed her hand and kissed it. She ripped her hand away from him and punched Al in the head.

He smiled broadly. "You are the essence of brilliance, Mademoiselle Two Face."

Tina rolled her eyes.

"Nice thinking, Tina," said Mega Bits. "A girl could go her whole life without seeing a Ponderosa Shake with a Texas Twist and a hint of Louisiana Shuffle. Well done."

I was going crazy. "What are you guys talking about? Nothing you've said makes any sense."

Eddie held his hand up at me, like a crossing guard trying to make me stop. "Al, can you and Sal paint your van green in the next twenty minutes?"

"I am offended that you would even ask such a thing. Part of being the best driver in the world is anticipating your every move."

"You already painted it?"

Al bowed. "Naturally."

Mega Bits squinted at the screen. "Looks like the van is headed to the other side of town. That should buy us a few more minutes."

I stood up, frustrated. "For the love of peanut butter, what are you guys talking about?!" I yelled.

Everybody stopped and stared at me.

"Haven't you been paying attention?" asked Spaghetti Eddie.

I stomped my foot. "Yes, and I don't have a clue what you're saying."

"It's simple, Lenny," said Eddie. "Mega Bits will track the peanut butter van from here and coordinate our movements, Al and Sal will pick up the fake peanut butter and get their green van into position while Tina prepares her part. Hey Tina, you think we need an ambulance?"

She shook her head. "Not enough time, just use whatever car is closest."

Eddie nodded. "Got it. Okay then, the only thing left is for me and you to find five hundred jars of fake peanut butter and intercept the blue suits and we need to do all of this in the next thirty minutes."

"But that's impossible," I said.

He grabbed my shoulder and shook. "Lenny, that's why you asked our help. Between Mega Bits, Two Faced Tina, Silent Sal, Annoying Al, Spaghetti Eddie, and you, we can handle this, okay?"

"Okay then. Actually, there is *one* more thing."

They all stared at me.

"Um, well, do you guys think I could have a nickname?"

Spaghetti Eddie looked at me then exchanged a peculiar look with Tina and Bits. "A nickname?"

"Yeah, right now I'm just Lenny and you guys all have these cool names. I was thinking something like The Peanut Butter Kid because I love peanut butter so much ... or maybe Long Socks Lenny cuz I like wearing long socks."

Spaghetti Eddie got an uncomfortable look on his face. "Yeah, not sure those nicknames work. Listen, Lenny, you're the one who pulled this crew together, you're the leader. A leader like you, you don't even need a nickname. You're just Lenny and that's okay."

"You sure?"

"Of course, plus, you don't need to be worrying about nicknames right now, you've got more important things to worry about because you my friend, are the Louisiana Shuffle."

CHAPTER SIXTEEN

For our Ponderosa Shake with a Texas Twist and a hint of Louisiana Shuffle to work, we were going to need five hundred hundred jars of fake peanut butter. When I asked why, I was told that it was all part of the Texas Twist of course. To obtain the fake peanut butter, Spaghetti Eddie pulled a large phone book out of his trench coat, flipped to a section labeled "Favorite Criminals" and dialed his phone. He then yelled at whoever was on the other end for about a minute. Finally, Eddie smiled. "Yep, just fill them with sand. Fine. But they have to have the peanut butter labels still on them, got it?" Eddie breathed a sigh of relief and hung up.

We grabbed earbud transmitters from Mega Bits and left the barn. Al and Sal were both a bit green from painting their van and were busy playing their brand of football. Al would yell "hike" and Sal would jump off the top of the van and dive for balls. We watched in astonishment as he caught five balls in a row. This guy was the Megatron of short Samoan criminal drivers.

Al was smiling, showing the green van off like Vanna White presenting letters on the *Wheel of Fortune*. We jumped in the van and Al and Sal roared that baby to life, peeled out of Granny's driveway, and rumbled through the neighborhood towards downtown. They dropped us off on Main Street, and Eddie hit the transmitter on his ear.

"Need a status update, Bits."

"Roger that, pasta boy. Blue Suit guys got held up with some rather wonky stop lights, the delay should help you out."

"You wouldn't be manipulating the street lights of Wedge City, now would you?" asked pasta boy.

I could almost hear Mega Bits smile through the transmitter. "Thought it was the least I could do. I'd say you have ten minutes before they come back your way."

"Keep us updated, over."

Eddie pointed at me. "Ten minutes—that gives us just enough time to prepare our part. We're going to need ourselves a car. He scanned the intersection and pointed. That one should do just fine."

Eddie walked over to an old blue four-door sedan parked in the all-day parking spot against the curb alongside the Sleepy Cafe. He pulled a long metal rod out of his trench coat, looked around to make sure no one was watching, and slid the metal thingy in between the door and the window of the car.

"Eddie," I said. "We can't steal a car."

He made a face. "Well, maybe you can't, but I can do this with my eyes closed. It's really quite easy once you get the hang of it."

"I mean it's not right to steal an innocent person's car."

He kept wiggling the bar inside the window. "Whether or not I agree with you on the particulars of that point, we don't actually need to steal this person's car. Just borrow it."

"What do you mean?" I asked.

"When Mega Bits gives us the signal, I'll pull this car into position. When we're done with the job, I'll pull it back into this spot."

"Really?" I said.

"Really," he said with a smile.

"And what again do you need me to do?"

"It's actually quite simple," said Eddie. Then he explained it. And I had to agree, it was simple. Stupid, but simple.

"But if Al and Sal have a van full of fake peanut butter, why do I need to steal the peanut butter from the back of the real van?"

I could tell Spaghetti was growing impatient. "Listen, Lenny. When you've pulled as many jobs as

I have, you learn that eventually, you just focus on your individual task. If all of us do our job, everything should work out. You'll see."

I wasn't so sure.

Mega Bit's voice crackled through my ear. "Okay, boys, three blocks away, no traffic in front of them near as I can tell, smooth sailing until your intersection. Have you heard from Al and Sal?"

Eddie looked at the time on his phone. "Not yet. They'll obviously be cutting it close, so do whatever else you can to stall the blue suits. Anything from Two Faced Tina?"

"Nothing yet," Bits responded.

"Roger that." Eddie looked concerned. He jumped into the car, bent low, looked like he was fiddling with something, then the car purred to life. Just like we'd discussed, I stood in the middle of the intersection while he carefully pulled it into position.

Bits piped in. "No can do on the delay boys. Blue suits at two hundred meters and closing fast. You better be in position now."

Eddie put the car in park, left the driver side door open and then ran to the front of the car and positioned himself on the ground. I ran across the street and hid behind a park bench, just like he'd instructed me.

I watched to my right as the van came our way. Two men filled the front seats, both wore silver sunglasses. I looked to my left. Eddie lay on the ground, squirming and moaning.

The van approached the intersection and stopped. Both of the blue suits looked at each other, then looked out the front windshield. They stared for a long time. Much longer than you should stare if someone in front of you had been run over by an old blue car. Finally, the driver opened his door and the passenger followed. They walked, then jogged to Eddie's side.

They fell for it.

Eddie was squirming, moaning. The blue suits knelt down next to him. From where I hid, he looked to be in terrible pain. Eddie's acting job was brilliant.

Even Two Faced Tina would be impressed. I crouched low, looked both ways to make sure nobody saw me, then sprinted for the back of their van.

"Okay, guys," Mega Bits said into my left ear. "Al just radioed in. We are right on schedule. Lenny, you sure you can do this?"

I'd been given one job in the Ponderosa Shake with a Texas Twist and a hint of Louisiana Shuffle. I was supposed to sneak around the back of the green van and start taking peanut butter. When I'd asked for an explanation of why I was doing this when we had a perfectly good van loaded up with fake peanut butter, Mega Bits just laughed. "Because it's got the hint of Louisiana Shuffle, duh?" Then Eddie told me to relax or he'd kick me in the stomach. Then he said to just worry about my job and it would all make sense in the end.

So that's what I was doing. Trusting a kid with a Mohawk, a bad attitude, and a rap sheet a mile long. A kid who loved spaghetti as much as I loved peanut butter. I would do my Louisiana Shuffle even though

I still didn't understand what the heck a Louisiana Shuffle even was.

I reached my hand up to the handle on the back of the van and gently opened it up. I looked inside.

After going days without a hint of peanut butter, I wasn't really prepared to be so close to so much of the greatest food in the world. It was awesome. And for a moment, I forgot why I was there.

"Lenny, do you copy?" came the voice from my earpiece. "Have you started?"

I reached in and grabbed my first jar of peanut butter. "Yes," I replied. I pulled open my pants and my jacket and began stuffing as much peanut butter in them as I could, just as Eddie had told me to do.

And that's when I heard the siren.

CHAPTER SEVENTEEN

I peeked my head out the back and saw a police car coming towards us fast. I crouched low in the back of the van and listened as the police car screeched to a stop. I froze.

"We got a problem, Bits."

This was not good. I stepped out of the van and peeked my head around the corner. The police officer, a short older man, was coming towards Spaghetti Eddie and did not look happy.

I touched the transmitter on my ear again. "Bits, we've got a major problem. Police are here."

"Just focus on your job, Lenny."

"Did you hear what I said? The police are here."

All of a sudden, Eddie sat up, screamed, then scrambled to his feet and sprinted away. The officer gave chase but only for a few feet before he put his hands on his knees, and, bent over, turned around.

Oh no.

"Bits, Eddie just left. Repeat, Spaghetti Eddie just fled the scene."

"Your job, Lenny," Bits growled through the transmitter. "Do your job."

I peaked around the corner of the van and now the officer was leading the two blue suits straight for me. I was out of time.

My survival instinct kicked in, and I sprinted away. But I couldn't get very far very fast with a bundle of peanut butter stuck in my drawers and that old cop must have been faster than I thought. Within seconds, he hit me in the back of the legs, and I fell forward and landed hard on my face. I tried to gather myself and scramble away, but the officer already had my left arm and violently yanked it behind my back.

"Ouch!" I yelled.

I felt something cold dig into my forearm and my other arm got yanked behind my arm.

"Ouch!" I yelled again.

I felt the cold metal of what I now knew were handcuffs being put on my other arm and then all of a sudden the officer got off my back and I tried to move.

But moving with your arms handcuffed behind your back is tricky. The officer helped me to my feet and spun me around.

He was short alright, probably mid-fifties with a large bushy mustache. The two men in the blue suits were next to him now.

"Yep," the officer said. "This boy was stealing peanut butter from the back of your van."

"What?" both blue suits said in unison.

The officer unzipped my jacket, yanked, and peanut butter fell out of my jacket and pants.

The officer waved his hands. "Oh yeah, we've seen this stunt before. One punk kid fakes an accident as a distraction while another punk kid comes in behind and starts stealing from the back of the vehicle." The cop over annunciated the word vehicle.

One of the blue suits started picking up the peanut butter that had fallen on the ground. The other looked down at his watch.

"Well, officer, I really appreciate this. However, we're on a deadline so can we be going now?"

The officer shook his head. "We all got deadlines, buddy. Unfortunately, I've got paperwork and you and your friend here have got to help me fill out some paperwork."

The driver threw his hands up in the air. "You've got to be kidding me."

I whispered into my transmitter. "A little help, Bits?"

The officer looked at me strangely then reached up to my ear and yanked my transmitter. He shook his head. "Obviously these punks are highly coordinated." He turned to the blues suits. "I suppose you'd like it if I just let this hooligan and his friends steal all your peanut butter next time. Would you rather that?"

The blue suit driver rolled his eyes. "Fine, but do we have to come down to the police station?"

The officer smiled and stabbed his finger their way. "Now here's where you're in luck. I can get all my information if we just step over to the sidewalk and into my mobile office." He held up his notepad and shook it. "Won't take more than a few minutes."

The blue suits agreed. The officer first led me to the police car, opened up the back door and shoved me inside. I then watched as he led the blue suits over to the sidewalk. The police officer leaned against the wall of a building with his notepad out, taking notes. The two blue suits answered questions, backs turned to the street.

And, I thought, this was it. The end of my childhood. The Colonel would be informed that his only son, the one who constantly disappoints him, had been arrested because he couldn't go without his precious peanut butter. The Colonel would fly home from saving the world, look at me with the world's most disappointing face, and then figure out how he could replace me with the shiny Army jeep that always performed up to Army standards. Up to his standards.

I was right in the middle of panicking, and sweating, and feeling my throat swell up like a wet sock, when I saw it. The green van belonging to the blue suits started to slowly move. At first, I thought I wasn't seeing straight. I looked over at the officer and the blue suits who were still answering questions. Then I looked back at the green van. The green van that was now, without a shadow of a doubt, moving away from the intersection and taking a left at the light.

What the heck?

I looked back at the officer and the blue suits. Their backs were turned and not one of them ever saw it. Then another flash of movement off to my right as another green van came down the street.

I watched as this van pulled right into the spot where the other van had sat.

And nobody but me saw a thing.

The officer held his pad up, nodded his head at the blue suits and shook both their hands. Then he came walking towards the police car. He opened up the driver's side door and stepped inside. He put the car in the ignition and turned the car on.

All of a sudden, the passenger side door opened, and a short kid with a mop of dark, curly hair climbed in.

"Silent Sal?" I said. He didn't answer me.

The Police officer moved to the passenger side as Silent Sal moved into the driver's seat.

He stretched his foot down to the pedal, peeked his head over the steering wheel, and pulled the cop car away. Halfway down the street, the police officer reached his fingers to the side of his face and dug them in and started to pull. As he did, his face began to slide off and then with a thoonk, his head just about popped off. Underneath that head was another head, belonging to a girl of twelve with short black hair. She shook her head like a dog after a bath and then turned around.

"Two faced Tina!" I said.

"Congratulations, Lenny, you're the brand new owner of five hundred jars of peanut butter."

 # CHAPTER EIGHTEEN

As I tried to piece together what exactly had just happened, and Tina laughed that I really didn't know what a Louisiana Shuffle was, Silent Sal drove the police car out of downtown and back to Megan's house. He parked it on the curb while Tina opened up the back door for me. She unlocked my handcuffs, and I shook my arms, trying to regain circulation.

"So that was all part of the plan?" I asked.

Tina smiled. "Well, of course it was. It isn't a Ponderosa Shake with a Texas Twist and a hint of Louisiana Shuffle without the hint of Shuffle."

"But nobody told me anything," I said.

Spaghetti Eddie, Mega Bits, and Annoying Al came running from the green van which was parked in the driveway. Al and Sal jumped into the air and chest bumped each other. Spaghetti Eddie punched me in the shoulder. "We know, Lenny, that's what makes the Shuffle so effective. You think you could have sold it if you knew? You may be the leader of this crew, but you're not exactly Two Faced Tina when it comes to your acting ability."

I looked at the green van. The real green van. "So it worked, we actually did it?"

Mega Bits smiled, her big teeth at their biggest. "You ready to see your haul?"

We walked over to the van. I opened up the back doors, climbed in, and grabbed a jar of peanut butter. I climbed out of the back, twisted off the cap, and stuck my nose in and took a deep, long whiff. My legs about buckled. I thought there was a chance I'd never see this delicious food spread ever again.

"Ahhhh," I said, a smile spreading across my face.

The crew looked at me and I felt my face getting warm. For a moment, I was embarrassed. Embarrassed that my unhealthy food obsession had led to, well, *all* of this. But right now, I didn't much care. I was hungry.

I dipped my finger into the peanut butter, and put it into my mouth.

"Peanut Butter."

"Taste good?" Bits asked.

"You can't even believe how good this tastes." I scooped another glob onto my finger, and slid it into my mouth. I think the crew got great amusement from watching me stuff my face with peanut butter for the next few minutes, but that's okay. They were all practically strangers to me, but for some reason, I didn't care about looking stupid in front of them.

Al and Sal appeared in front of us, Sal tossing a football up into the air, and Al catching it.

"My brother and I have a tradition," Al said at his normal super speed. Incredibly, I'd begun to understand him. "After every successful job, we play a game of football."

Sal looked at Granny's large front yard and nodded.

Tina cracked her knuckles. "I wouldn't mind messing you fools up." Bits shrugged. "Me too."

"Okay then," Spaghetti Eddie said.

But I thought of something.

"Hey, guys, you said when we finished our job you might consider a nickname for me."

Eddie and Tina exchanged another weird look. "Lenny, just cool it with the nickname okay," Eddie said. He grabbed the football from Al. "All I want you to do right now is go long. Let's see if just Lenny can catch a football."

Eddie pumped the football, and I took off. I felt great, better than I had every felt in my life. The combination of pulling that job, and filling my stomach with peanut butter had given me the energy of a cheetah. And I felt just as fast. Eddie heaved the ball into the air and I ran for it. At the last moment I jumped, and ran smack dab into a short hedge. I fell over it into a heap.

I heard the crew laugh behind me. Then I heard something else: tires screeching violently. I looked up over the hedge and two black SUV's skidded in front of Granny's driveway. Six enormous goons jumped out. I knew those guys.

They were on top of my friends before any of them knew what had happened. They had Mega Bits, Al, Sal, Two Faced Tina, and Spaghetti Eddie in their enormous paws. And my old friend, Mr. Personal guard himself had his head on a swivel, looking around.

And he found me.

As soon as he spotted me behind the hedge, he came charging like a bull. But I was too fast. That little bit of peanut butter, plus my desire not to die as a twelve year old, gave me super speed. I ran into the neighbor's backyard, hopped a fence, and ran for the next ten minutes without ever looking back.

When I was certain I'd lost him, I collapsed to the ground until I caught my breath. And when I thought I could move again, I stood upright and walked. And once again, I was alone. And I'd never, ever, felt more alone than I did at that exact moment.

 # CHAPTER NINETEEN

I walked through our front door and saw my mom ten feet in front of me, folding clothes. Her expression changed as soon as she saw me. My mom knew me too well.

She dropped her clothes and stood up. "What happened?"

"I don't want to talk about it." I tried to walk past her but she stopped me. She held me by the shoulders and looked at me.

"Lenny Parker, what happened?"

"I said I don't want to talk about it, okay?" I shook her off and I saw at once that I'd hurt her feelings. She took a breath that moved her shoulders up and down.

"It's just—you've been so happy for the last couple of days, it's been nice to see."

"I have?"

"Yes, Lenny, you have. I guess I was hoping something was different."

I thought about Mega Bits, and Spaghetti Eddie, and the rest of the crew. For the first time in forever, I'd felt part of something, like maybe, just maybe, I might have friends.

That was, of course, a colossal mistake. I had forgotten my number one rule. Never, ever make friends. It always ends in disappointment.

And that disappointment was all because of the Colonel.

I growled. "I hate everything about the Army."

My mom stiffened. "You don't mean that."

My face was warm and my throat was tight. "Yes, I do. I hate it. I wish Dad was never part of it. All he does is talk about the Army way and all he does is spend time with them. Not with us, Mom. With them! All he does is fly overseas and save the world. How about spending time with you and me and taking me to a San Francisco Giants game and maybe, just maybe being a family. How about that, Mom!?"

My throat hurt. My cheeks were wet with tears. My whole body was tensed up like a clenched fist.

My mom sat down and folded her hands in her lap. "So that's really the way you feel?"

I nodded.

"Lenny, I know your dad can be hard sometimes, and I know he's gone a lot. Trust me, I know. And I know you don't want to hear what I'm about to say, but I have to tell you something. Your father would never tell you this story because he didn't even tell me. One of his men did."

"I'm not really in the mood."

"Frankly, Lenny, I don't care if you're in the mood. Just listen."

I nodded.

"When your father was a young lieutenant, four of the men in his platoon got pinned down in a fierce gun battle. They were on some sort of very important mission. Your father's job was to keep going and carry out the mission. But your father? He couldn't just leave his men behind. So, he sent the rest of the platoon forward to finish the mission and he went back, alone, behind enemy lines to rescue those four men. During this battle, your father was shot, but he saved three of those men that day. Those men had wives and children and he saved them and they're alive today because of it."

I swallowed hard.

"And what about the fourth man?"

Mom shook her head. "He didn't make it. Turns out he threw himself on a grenade to save your father, and that's why he never told me about it. That man was your father's best friend. Your father saved those men that day and his best friend saved him."

I hung my head and the tears came back.

"Lenny, I don't want to make you feel bad, but that's why your father does what he does. He feels he has a duty, to his men, to all men in uniform, to never ever leave a man behind. It's not that he loves you less, it's that he's trying so hard to love so many. And it's tough to do."

Mom looked at me with her own fiery love, then she picked up her laundry basket and walked upstairs. I sat down on the couch.

So my dad really *was* a hero. My dad was the reason other dads had kids. Kids like me. Because he never left a man behind.

I wondered if I would ever be like my dad. And then, like an arrow to my heart, it hit me. Maybe I couldn't be just like my dad, but maybe I could start.

Dad was a hero because he never left a man behind and right now, I'd left my men, my crew behind.

Maybe I could start right now.

I stood, left the house, jumped on my bike and tore off down the street. I knew exactly what I had to do.

CHAPTER TWENTY

I rode my bike to Pellano's Restaurant. As one of the guards came towards me, I picked up my bike and tossed it to him. "Take good care of it, okay?" The other one, my old friend personal guard was licking his lips. He brought his mighty paw down on my shoulder and I knocked it away and then kicked him hard in the shin.

"Why you little—"

"I came to see Scar."

The guard holding my bike looked at the one holding his shin smirked. "Your funeral kid."

He put his hand on my back to guard me through the door and I again knocked it away. "I remember how to get there, okay?"

The scents of spaghetti sauce hit me as I entered the restaurant, and just like last time, the heavy set Italian woman was on the phone looking cross. I walked up the stairs and the guard at the door raised his eyebrows when he saw me.

"I want to see Scar."

The guard tilted his head. "And he most definitely wants to see you."

I walked in to a packed dining hall, with large men in dark suits once again slopping down spaghetti like pigs at a food trough. One of the guys next to Scar saw me, then nudged Scar who looked at me, and dropped his fork. He stood up and the room went dead quiet except for one late fork screeching against a china plate.

"I thought we had a deal," Scar said.

"We did," I replied. "I put together a crew and we stole five hundred jars of peanut butter. One day earlier than we had to, mind you."

Scar shook his head. "The deal," he roared, "was that you were supposed to steal that peanut butter without those blue suits knowing anything about it."

"And we did, we switched their van for ours and they had no idea."

"Except that two hours ago, I get a call from a very important guy, and he says 'Scar, I thought you were gonna leave the peanut butter alone?'"

"They found out?" I said.

"Yeah, they did. Apparently, when those blue suits reached their destination, they found a bunch of jars of sand with no peanut butter labels."

I clenched my fists. *They forgot the labels.*

"And you made me look bad, kid. I couldn't exactly tell this guy that I sanctioned the job so, instead, I look weak, like I can't control my own town." Scar cracked his knuckles. "I don't like to look weak, so now someone's got to pay."

He waved his hand and one of his guys opened up a back door. Silent Sal came in first, followed by Annoying Al, Two Faced Tina, Spaghetti Eddie, and lastly Mega Bits. All of them were tied up, and had handkerchiefs wrapped around their mouths. None of them looked particularly glad to see me.

And I couldn't blame them because it was my fault they were in this mess.

A couple guards led them over the trap door. Mega Bits stood on the red 'x' and the crew gathered around her.

Scar licked his lips. "Like I said, Lenny, someone's got to pay."

Mega Bits looked back at me with her crazy hair and big teeth. She'd reached out to me, was kind to me, when she didn't have to. Now she stood over a trap door that led to, well, I had no idea. Just no place good.

"Mr. Scar, your deal was with me." I stepped up to the trap door and pushed Mega Bits and the rest of the crew away. I stood as straight and tall as I could. Like the Colonel taught me to do for inspection. Army standards. The Colonel standards.

I puffed out my chest. "If anybody's going to pay, it's got to be me. Now let my crew go."

Scar chuckled. "Why should I?"

"Because you may be a criminal, but I'm willing to bet you're an honorable criminal. You let them go, and make me suffer the consequences instead."

Scar danced his tongue along his lip and then nodded to his guards. They untied my crew and then took the gags off.

"Don't do this, Lenny," Bits yelled.

But it was too late. The guards dragged my friends away.

There I said it, my *friends*.

At least, I hoped they could be my friends.

Turns out not having friends is hard, about the hardest thing in the world.

Even harder than having a dad gone all the time saving the world.

Scar clapped his huge hands together. "So you know what this means, right kid?"

"The trap door?"

"And you're willing to do it?" Scar said.

"I guess I don't have a choice."

Scar looked around. "We all got choices, Lenny."

"I guess I've made mine."

He made a face. "Pity. I really wish things could have been different. You got any last words?"

I swallowed. "Last words?" I said.

"Yeah, something nice about your mom, prayer to the baby Jesus. That type a thing?"

I wasn't much for words. So I had thoughts instead. I thought about my sweet mom, I thought about the San Francisco Giants, I thought about my friends, and I thought about the Colonel. My dad.

I missed my dad.

"You sure you're willing to take the trap door to save your crew?" said Scar.

I thought of something the Colonel said one time about baseball. If you go down, better to go down swinging.

"You know, Mr. Scar, your Goldfish has one really, really disgusting eye."

He growled and shook the rectangular table. "Nobody, and I mean nobody stares at my goldfish."

I clenched my body. "Well, looks like I just did."

He slipped his hand under the table and I closed my eyes. The floor went out from underneath me and I fell.

CHAPTER TWENTY-ONE

I expected the sharp pointy spikes of a mob boss torture device to poke me or the slimy stomach of an ancient monster to devour me. Instead, I landed on something hard and smooth and began sliding fast through a tunnel of darkness. Seriously, I couldn't see anything as I catapulted through a tunnel that I was certain was probably the throat of a dragon and incredibly, I continued to pick up more and more speed. Finally, the darkness broke as I saw a little crack of light and as I got closer, I screamed as I got shot out of a hole and went flying through the air. I landed in a terrible smelling mess and for a moment was certain I'd landed in the soft underbelly of Hades.

But only for a moment.

Something gross and slimy was in my mouth and I tried to spit it out. I turned around and noticed I was in an alley.

An alley in my world. I was alive and I was in an alley.

Not an Italian torture chamber or a great dragon's stomach. An alley, a regular old alley with trash, and rats, and sunshine, and freedom, and life.

I yelled at the top of my lungs.

And in the distance I heard a response.

"Lenny?" someone yelled back. I looked down the alley and my crew was there. My friends. They came sprinting for me.

"Lenny!" Spaghetti Eddie screamed as he skateboarded my way.

"You're alive!" Mega Bits yelled as she jumped in the air. Sal and Al chest bumped and for once, Tina didn't look so angry.

I felt my body. Bits was right. I *was* alive. And, by the smell of myself, also incredibly disgusting. I spit more slimy stuff out of my mouth. Every inch of my body felt like it was covered in goop and muck and grime. Like I'd taken a bath in a mixture of yogurt and poop.

But at the moment, I didn't much care.

"You came back and you saved us," said Mega Bits, smiling so broad her big teeth looked like Walrus tusks.

"But I ran away and left you first," I said.

"Doesn't matter, Lenny," said Tina. "You came back. You took the trap door for us."

Annoying Al bowed. "I am forever in debt to you, Mr. Lenny."

Silent Sal stepped forward and held out his hand. I took it and he squeezed.

I all of a sudden became aware of something very slimy stuck to the side of my face. I started to shake. "W-what the heck is this guys?" I pointed.

"Looks like bologna," said Mega Bits.

"Or smoked ham," said Tina.

"My bet's on oven roasted turkey," said Eddie.

"What are you talking about?" I said.

Spaghetti Eddie stepped forward and ripped it off. He showed it to me. "Relax, it's just lunchmeat, Lenny."

I breathed a sigh of relief, and then Eddie made a face.

"Lunchmeat Lenny," he said again out loud to no one in particular. Then his mouth grew into a big smile, and he turned around. He brought the crew together for a huddle. Then finally he popped his head up and they all turned around.

"Lunchmeat Lenny!" he practically yelled.

"I don't understand," I said.

"You wanted a nickname, and now you've got it. A great nickname for a great leader. Lunchmeat Lenny."

"Lunchmeat Lenny?" I said.

"Lunchmeat Lenny," the crew responded.

A honk caught my attention. A black SUV was driving slowly down the alley. A large scary man stepped out of the back.

Scar Pellano.

He stepped towards me. "You know kid, you're the first person who ever took the trap door voluntarily."

"I am?"

"Yes, you are. That took guts kid. You may have screwed up our deal, but you showed me something back there. You stepped up for your crew. That took courage, and that's what a real leader needs. So guess what? You passed the test."

"I did?" I said.

"Yeah. The boys took half of the peanut butter which means you and your friends got one green van and two hundred and fifty jars of peanut butter to play with."

"Thanks, Mr. Scar. Thanks a lot."

"Don't mention it. But here's the other thing. You and your crew now got permission to operate in

Wedge City. I've been looking for a crime boss to look over my middle school interests and I've found one in you."

A crime boss? "Sorry, Scar, but I think there's been a misunderstanding. I don't want to be a crime boss."

Scar looked around. "You calling me stupid, kid?"

"No, not at all, It's just I don't want to—"

"Cuz it sounds to me like you're calling me stupid," said Scar. "You want to find out what I do to people who call me stupid?"

"No sir, Mr. Scar."

"Good. Like I said, Lenny—"

Spaghetti Eddie interrupted. "It's actually Lunchmeat Lenny."

Scar scrunched his chin up. "I like it. You, Lunchmeat Lenny, are my new middle school crime boss. You keep an eye out for me and let me know what's going on. Got it?"

I couldn't believe this was happening. But Scar had made it pretty clear that I didn't have much of a choice.

"I got it."

CHAPTER TWENTY-TWO

Turns out, once you get rid of all the peanut butter in the world, stolen peanut butter suddenly becomes very valuable. Eddie helped me find a buyer for my stolen goods and with the proceeds, I was able settle some debts.

By a great stroke of luck, the Pittsburgh Steelers were in Northern California that Sunday to play the San Francisco Forty-Niners. After contacting the *California Samoans for Polamalu Fan Club*, I was not only able to buy Al and Sal a pair of tickets to the game, but I was also able to arrange a meeting with their favorite player, Troy Polamalu.

Handling my debt with Two Faced Tina was a little trickier, at least at first. She wanted to play Ebenezer Scrooge in the next production of the Christmas Carol. But Elliot Turnbull had been virtually guaranteed the part for life. At first, Mega Bits suggested the whole poison idea again. Spaghetti Eddie thought we might just be able to kidnap him until after the New Year. But I settled on a much more legal approach. Turns out actors in the community theatre don't get paid, and Mr. Turnbull was quite tired of that arrangement. So I paid him off and he gladly called the director of the play and recommended the wonderfully-talented Tina Miaki for the part.

Spaghetti Eddie continued to get out of detention whenever he liked and thus far, Helmet Kruger hadn't figure it out. And after much shopping online, Mega Bits finally picked out the fancy doohickey electronic gizmo she'd always wanted. I couldn't pronounce the name of it and had no idea what it actually did, but it was really expensive and Mega Bits was happy.

And I was happy as well. I was poor, but happy. Paying off my debts had forced me to sell almost all of my peanut butter. In the end, I had only seven jars left. And, worried that I might never get my hands on another jar again, I hid those seven jars under my bed.

How did I live without the world's perfect food? Well, I'd proven some things to myself. I'd proven I could go without peanut butter. I'd also proven that I could find other foods to eat. And after finding my crew, I thought maybe I had found some kids who could actually be my friends.

Maybe this town and this time could be different after all?

And that's when Mom got the call that the Colonel was finally coming home from his overseas trip.

I was in the living room when he arrived. He gave my mom a big hug and then, like he always did, straightened up and the two of us saluted each other.

He smiled a big broad smile. "Well, folks, I for one, am hungry. What do we got for food in this house?"

Mom smiled. "Well, Lenny was just in the kitchen making sandwiches," she said.

The Colonel rolled his eyes then sighed with disappointment. "Okay, fine."

I walked into the kitchen first, and grabbed a sandwich off my plate. The colonel looked at the other two plates and he got a strange look on his face.

I smiled, then took a huge bite out of my turkey and ham sandwich. The Colonel's mouth fell open. Then he pointed at me. I do believe the Colonel was kind of speechless.

"But, but, but that's ... that's lunchmeat, Lenny!"

I took another big bite and smiled back at my dad.

"Yes," I said with pride. "Yes, it is."

Well, there's my explanation for how I came to be known as Lunchmeat Lenny and how I found my extraordinary crew. I suppose you're still wondering about that picture on the front of the book, aren't you? A day after the Colonel returned home, Spaghetti Eddie said our little crew needed some business cards. He made up a card that said Lunchmeat Lenny 6th Grade Crime Boss, *Don't Call Us, We'll Call You.* There was just one little problem. The kid representing Lunchmeat Lenny didn't look anything like me. When I asked Eddie about it, he shrugged. "No offense Lenny, but you're not the most intimidating kid in the world and this crew and its leader should strike fear in the hearts of people."

"But won't people figure it out when they actually meet me?" I asked after thinking that through for a moment.

"Nah," Eddie said. "I'll just tell them that's what you look like when you get angry. And they don't want to make you angry."

THE END

Can you help me spread the word about **Lunchmeat Lenny 6th Grade Crime Boss**? If you enjoyed reading about Lenny, Mega Bits, Spaghetti Eddie, Two Faced Tina, Annoying Al, and Silent Sal, then I would be honored if you asked a parent to help you write a short review about my book on Amazon.com. Those honest reviews really help readers find my books, and I want to introduce Lunchmeat Lenny and his crew to as many readers as possible.

Thank you so much!

ALSO WRITTEN BY DANIEL KENNEY

When Peter Mills descends into the creepy basement of Finley Junior High, he discovers a dark and twisted truth: girls haven't always ruled the world.

Now armed with a book of ancient, forbidden man secrets (such as how to make paper airplanes, stink bombs, and beef jerky), Peter and his friends think they've found the recipe to changing their lives. But the boys of the Beef Jerky Gang will soon find out that the girls aren't about to give up control to a bunch of prank-pulling punks.

Join Peter and his friends in this hilarious first book of the Beef Jerky Gang series.

To buy the book go to Amazon.com.

WRITTEN BY DANIEL KENNEY AND EMILY BOEVER

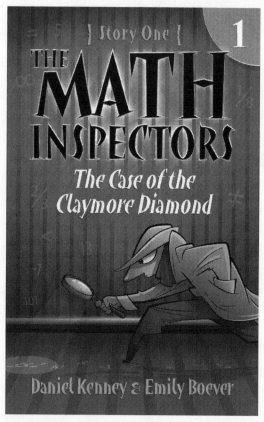

When the Claymore Diamond is stolen from Ravensburg's finest jewelry store, Stanley Carusoe gets the bright idea that he and his friends should start a detective agency.

Armed with curiosity and their love for math, Stanley, Charlotte, Gertie, and Felix race around town in an attempt to solve the mystery. Along the way, they butt heads with an ambitious police chief, uncover dark secrets, and drink lots of milkshakes at Mabel's Diner. But when their backs are against the wall, Stanley and his friends rely on the one thing they know best: numbers. Because numbers, they never lie.

Join Stanley and his friends in this smart and funny first mystery in The Math Inspectors series, perfect for math lovers, math haters, and all kids ages 9-12.

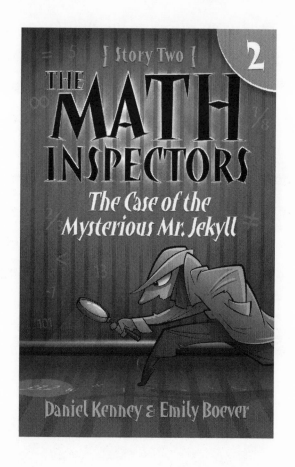

Sixth-graders Stanley, Charlotte, Gertie and Felix did more than just start a detective agency. Using their math skills and gut instincts, they actually solved a crime the police couldn't crack.

Now, the Math Inspectors are called in to uncover the identity of a serial criminal named Mr. Jekyll, whose bizarre (and hilarious) pranks cross the line into vandalism. But the deeper the friends delve into the crimes, the more they realize why they were asked to help... and it wasn't because of their detective skills.

Join Stanley and his friends in another thrilling adventure of the Math Inspectors series, perfect for math lovers, math haters, and all kids ages 9-12.

To learn more visit www.TheMathInspectors.com.

ABOUT THE AUTHOR

DANIEL KENNEY

Daniel Kenney and his wife Teresa live in Omaha, Nebraska with zero cats, zero dogs, one gecko and lots of kids. When those kids aren't driving him nuts, Daniel is busy writing books, cheering on the Benedictine Ravens, and plotting to take over the world. He is the author of The Beef Jerky Gang series, the co-author of The Math Inspectors series, and the author of several other stories and books. Find more information at www.DanielKenney.com

Made in the USA
Charleston, SC
21 January 2015